TED TAYLER

FINAL DEAL

BOOKS

By Ted Tayler

The Freeman Files

Fatal Decision

Last Orders

Pressure Point

Deadly Formula

Final Deal

Barking Mad

Creature Discomforts

Silent Terror

Night Train

All Things Bright

Buried Secrets

A Genuine Mistake

Strange Beginnings

Dead Reckoning

A Normal November

Into the Sunlight

Tame the Storm

One True Friend

Whispered Truths

A Morning Murder

Quick to Anger

Red Herring Season

Gathering Clouds

Still Standing

Vinci Books

vinci-books.com

Published by Vinci Books Ltd in 2025

1

Paperback ISBN: 9781036704919

Chapter One

Friday, 18 May 2018

DI SUZIE FERRIS woke to the sound of her alarm.

Today was her last day at the College of Policing before returning to Devizes. The call she received from the Chief Constable ten days ago came as a complete surprise. Suzie was about to drive into the London Road HQ to start the week after the Bank Holiday.

Her thoughts at the time centred on Gus Freeman and whether she would see him later. Suzie expected Gus to report to the ACC and Geoff Mercer about his team's progress in Swindon. She prayed things wouldn't be awkward if they bumped into one another.

The events of the fourth of May, followed by a passionate Saturday morning, meant Gus remained conflicted, but Suzie's feelings were crystal clear. She wanted Gus in her life, no matter what problems it raised.

Back in the real world on Tuesday, Sandra Plunkett

informed Suzie she had enrolled her on a Digital and Cyber-crime course at Ryton-on-Dunsmore, near Coventry. The Chief Constable also gave strict instructions that mobile phones and laptops were not permitted. She told Suzie to leave her communication devices at home.

On her two-hour drive to the Midlands on the A429, Suzie split the journey time between thoughts of Gus and wondering why this course at the College of Policing had never surfaced before today.

Geoff Mercer was her immediate superior. Her career improvement initiatives came through him in the usual scheme of things. Perhaps the Chief Constable knew about her and Gus and wanted to keep them at arm's length.

Suzie had told herself not to be daft. It was their secret, and that's the way it stayed.

After a tiring day at College last Friday, Suzie called her mother from her hotel room in the evening and said she decided to stay in Coventry over the weekend. There were several course attendees from the West Midlands force, and with plenty of live music venues, party bars and nightclubs available, it offered a chance to relax with her colleagues.

The aim of a hedonist weekend was not to get Gus Freeman out of her system; far from it, Suzie needed to keep active to stop pining for him.

On Saturday morning, after a boozy night, Suzie wished she was back home to take her usual horse ride across the fields near Worton. Fresh air always helped clear a thick head. She spent the morning in recovery mode.

After a light lunch, Suzie drove to King's Norton for the Farmer's Market. She'd spotted an advert online weeks ago, and this course offered a perfect opportunity to fit in a visit. Two dozen producers displayed their wares on brightly coloured stalls. The site soon filled with families and couples wandering from stall to stall, enjoying the sights and sounds of rural England.

Everything reminded her of the community spirit that flourished in the Wiltshire countryside she called home. The walk did her good. Suzie prepared for another night on the town.

Most of Sunday, Suzie spent in bed, under the covers. Even with the curtains drawn, the bright sunlight hurt her eyes. Suzie had recovered by Monday morning when she returned to the College to start the final five days of the course.

Now, on this overcast Friday morning, only a half-day wrap-up session remained before everyone said their farewells and headed home for the weekend. Time ticked on, so Suzie jumped out of bed and took a shower.

There hadn't been many opportunities to use her car since she'd been in the Midlands. Still, a glance at her petrol gauge yesterday evening suggested a visit to a garage for petrol would be best before embarking on the two-hour journey home.

Suzie wondered what Gus was doing this morning as she towelled herself dry. She wanted to call him. It was so frustrating not having her mobile phone. Everyone else had access to theirs in the evenings and weekends when she met them. It made no sense.

During the day, the busy schedule left little spare time for checking messages or social media, and every guest speaker reminded people of the ban on mobiles in the lecture halls. What the heck, thought Suzie. The course will be over by lunchtime, and I can get back to Wiltshire and call Gus as soon as I get home.

With her bags packed and dressed to impress for her last day, Suzie checked out and left the hotel for the last time.

She drove towards Ryton-on-Dunsmore, stopping at a garage to fill her Golf GTI's tank with petrol. She glanced at the pump number and crossed the forecourt to pay.

The garage's mini-supermarket had several customers in the queue, and Suzie waited her turn to reach the counter. She spotted a Costa Coffee franchise in the far corner with a tall, angular man with his back to her.

Suzie resisted the temptation to dash over to buy a large latte. She couldn't stand those people who wandered into work carrying a giant container of overpriced liquid. Why didn't they get out of bed earlier and have a decent break-fast before they left home?

The queue moved forward, and Suzie forgot the man lingering on the far side of the shop. Once she'd paid for her petrol, she left and walked to her car. As she pulled off the forecourt into traffic, she spotted a black van forcing its way into the queue behind her.

How inconsiderate, Suzie thought. What can they hope to gain? Everyone has to wait for a gap in heavy rush-hour traffic. There's no panic. Fifteen minutes later, she pulled into the College entrance. The black van followed her two cars back. Suzie slowed as she turned left into the car park and glanced across at the driver's cab. She should have guessed. The driver was that tall angular-looking guy, maybe in his fifties, who had stood by the coffee machine earlier. Suzie thought he stared straight at her.

As she parked in a bay reserved for course attendees, she recognised a girl she'd befriended over the weekend. Suzie gathered her things from the passenger seat, hopped out and locked her car.

"Hi, Josie," she called.

"Not long before we can get back to the humdrum life of crime we've missed so much," grinned Josie Bennett.

"This cyber-crime stuff is so different from the reality I face on the streets surrounding the old nick in Bordesley Green."

"I guess they staff that relic of Victorian grandeur with community police these days?" asked Suzie.

"A uniformed Sergeant, a handful of Constables and the rest are PCSOs," said Josie, "everything major gets organised from Snow Hill."

"Did you grow up around Bordesley Green?" asked Suzie, keeping a weather eye on the black van.

The vehicle was stationary, engine idling and not yet sited in a parking bay.

"Growing up isn't the word I would use. My parents dragged me up, more like it. My experience in an inner-city borough wasn't idyllic. Not like you in the rolling countryside."

"You mean for us soft Southerners? It was different growing up on a farm, I grant you, but not a bed of roses. Unless you've worked on a large farm and realise how much work goes into keeping your head above water daily, it's hard to compare. You had to grow up fast because you lived on an estate of so-called mean streets. So my brothers and I grew up fast, watching calves and lambs struggle to survive in the first few hours after we'd help deliver them into the world. Every lost animal became an emotional punch in the gut. We soon learned that clothes, the toy we craved, and a replacement for the clapped-out tractor our father coaxed into daily life relied on us to salvage all the little mites we could."

"Alright, keep your hair on. We never had a Pony Club on our doorstep, though. Let's change the subject. How have you got on with your new Chief Constable?" asked Josie as they reached the front door.

"She's as hard as nails," said Suzie, "which is understandable. It's the only way a woman can be if she wants to reach the top."

"You don't want to get on the wrong side of her," said Josie, "Sandra can be a right bitch. It goes with the territory, I guess, although her partner is a pussy cat. When they socialised with us, which wasn't often, the guys called them Butch and Sundance."

The two DIs paused inside the building as Josie nodded towards a group of male course attendees trotting across the car park towards them.

"Cutting it fine, as usual," she laughed, "and yet they'll still get further than you and I with the promotion boards."

"Not if I can help it," said Suzie. "Did you see that black van in the car park?"

"I never noticed one. Why?" said Josie.

"A van followed me here. I'm sure of it. The driver was alone at the garage, where I filled up, getting a coffee. I'd never seen him before."

"Either he fancied you, or he lost his way. You would need some nerve to enter this car park if you weren't a copper unless you had a good reason to be here. The signs are big enough. He's gone now, hasn't he? Why worry?"

Suzie shrugged. Josie was probably right.

Three hours later, the course ended, and groups gathered to say their goodbyes and make empty promises to keep in touch. Suzie collected a few phone numbers in her notebook.

"Did you leave your phone in the car?" asked Josie as they swapped numbers.

"I was told not to bring any communication devices; no mobiles or laptops permitted, according to my Chief Constable."

"No way," said Josie, pulling a face, "none of us got that message. Perhaps she fancies you. Or are you sleeping with one of your ACCs, and she wanted to put a spoke in your wheel?"

Suzie hoped the heat she felt at that remark didn't show on her face.

"I thought my behaviour over the weekend convinced you I enjoy a good time as much as the next single girl," she replied. "I'm thirty-three. There are no women in my life, and I've had fun without wanting to marry any of the men I've dated yet."

"Sandra Plunkett may have the right idea for reaching the top in this game," said Josie. "Somehow, I don't see her needing children to complete the family unit. I'm two years younger than you and want to get married and have kids. But, when I look at the men I come into contact with, it doesn't fill me with optimism."

"I made the mistake of trying to turn the clock back a few weeks ago," said Suzie as she and Josie stood by Suzie's car. "An old boyfriend moved back into the area and got in touch. He played professional rugby for several years. Now he's a player-coach with a local club. He's not a copper nor a criminal, but it was a disaster."

"Can you remember his number? I'll stick it on my phone. If you don't have any further use for him, I enjoy a scrum-down now and again."

"I can't recall it at the minute," said Suzie, "when I get home and get reunited with my mobile, I'll forward his details."

Josie gave Suzie a quick hug and headed towards her car. Suzie called after her.

"Just make sure you never forget his name."

Suzie was already motoring out of the car park. Josie

stood with her hand on her door handle with a bemused look.

"I wonder what that was about?" she thought, jumping into the driver's seat and looking forward to another hectic weekend.

AS SUZIE FERRIS negotiated the early afternoon traffic between the College and the quickest route south to Wiltshire, Gus Freeman and DS Alex Hardy were going to Salisbury. They met with Clive Breakwell at the research establishment where Dr Ian McGuire used to work. Breakwell and McGuire were friends and colleagues.

Gus knew Suzie was attending a course in the Midlands, but his lack of success in getting a reply to his text messages troubled him more than he wanted to admit. He hated not being able to give total concentration to a meeting. Gus hoped Alex Hardy picked up any crumbs of valuable information he missed this afternoon.

Clive Breakwell told them of a break-in at the lab between Christmas and New Year 2003. The burglars stole McGuire's laptop containing a deadly formula for crystal meth. The break-in fitted with the subsequent deaths of two of Kai Belafonte's cousins. Those deaths resulted from the high purity of a batch of crystal meth achieved by Ian McGuire. The scientist was proving to himself that his genius was undiminished. He destroyed the test batch and forgot about the experiment. However, the laptop retained details of the formula, and the thieves were unaware of the price they would pay for playing with fire.

Kai's half-brother Jax Jackson supplied the weapon and ammunition the fourteen-year-old used to get his revenge.

He climbed over the fence behind McGuire's home, crept to the patio, and shot the scientist through the window.

When Gus left Salisbury later that afternoon, he knew the identity of McGuire's killer. Finally, another open cold case could close after a fourteen-year gap. But, even as he left the research lab, Gus Freeman wondered whether unmasking the killer was the right thing to do.

While Alex and Gus returned to the CRT office, Suzie was nearing Royal Leamington Spa, the Regency town famed for its wide boulevards, Georgian architecture and beautiful parks. She'd tuned her car radio to the local station to catch traffic alerts when she travelled from her hotel daily. Suzie thanked her lucky stars she'd forgotten to switch channels. There was a fifteen-mile tailback on the M5 below Junction 6 near Worcester. That was where she planned to join the motorway, with her ultimate destination being the Bath junction on the M4. There weren't many better places to shop when you had a spare afternoon.

Suzie did a quick re-jig of her trip home. She could take advantage of the opportunity to shop here in the Spa town. The place had a reputation for excellent food, and with Royal Priors and Regent Court shopping centres within a stone's throw of a large car park, it was ideal. If the tailback eased by three o'clock, she'd join the M5 as planned. If not, she'd take the more leisurely A429 route as she had when she came north.

She forgot the unwanted attention of the stranger this morning. Suzie saw plenty of black vans on the roads, but none gave her cause for concern. She spent two pleasant hours eating a light lunch and strolling through various department stores. It was impossible to avoid making a few purchases.

A girl can never have too many shoes. Suzie also bought

more underwear. Her mother always warned her never to go out without a clean pair in case she was in an accident.

Suzie would have returned to her car twenty minutes earlier if it wasn't for a handbag dilemma. She eyed it in the shop window of a famous brand, and it was just the right size and colour—something she'd wanted for ages. Inside the shop, Suzie held it, hung it over her shoulder and admired the look in the mirror. It was expensive. Should she splash out and buy it? There was just one tiny niggle. The strap wasn't adjustable. If Suzie were six feet tall, it would be perfect. Any attempt to shorten the strap would be apparent. The design only worked with the strap as it was. In the end, Suzie admitted defeat.

Suzie hurried back to the multi-storey car park. She wanted to check the traffic situation before deciding which road to take out of town. She darted up the stairwell to the First Floor and strode towards her Golf GTI.

Car parks aren't the safest places for women alone, but Suzie felt secure enough in the middle of the afternoon. The low ceilings would make this place much scarier late in the evening. Suzie looked to her left and right. She could see nobody close by her.

It was eerily quiet, and Suzie sighed with relief when she saw the boot of her car in the bay beyond the next pillar. She was thankful the architect opted for wider bays than average. Suzie rummaged in her handbag for her keys and gathered her purchases into the same hand while she opened the door.

She sensed movement behind her and froze. Her feet swept from under her, and a firm shove pitched Suzie forward onto her knees. Her shopping slid under the rear of the GTI. On the floor, Suzie realised she was dealing with a single attacker. The man dragged her to her feet and frogmarched her towards a vehicle opposite. The rear doors were open, and her attacker bundled her into the back of a black van.

It had to be the man from the garage. She'd not spotted him all afternoon. Despite her training, Suzie realised resistance was pointless.

Inside the van, the man placed a cloth bag loosely over her head, holding her in a tight headlock face down, making it hard to breathe. He flipped her onto her back like a rag doll, and she felt the cold steel of a handcuff clamped onto her right wrist.

Her instinct was to kick out and punch her attacker with her left arm, but she encountered nothing but fresh air. He had moved out of reach. Suzie realised the other handcuff was now securing her to the side of the van. There was no escape. She heard the back doors slam shut. At first, there was silence, and then a minute later, they were on the move.

Who was he, and what did he want? Where was he taking her?

Suzie tried to think as she sat on the floor of the van. They were out of the car park and in traffic within a minute. What time was it when he kidnapped her? She thought it must have been three o'clock. Suzie listened to the van's engine sound and the frequency with which they slowed or stopped.

The way the van was travelling, they were still in a built-up area. That meant there were traffic lights, roundabouts, and a pedestrian crossing. She could hear the beeps indicating it was safe to cross. Suzie yelled for help, but nobody could hear her cries. The van was on the move again.

Progress was smoother now, and they were travelling at speed. Did that mean they were on a major road, dual carriageway, or motorway? Suzie cursed. If only this had happened near her home. She might recognise where they were. She had planned to head for the M5 near Worcester when her captor struck. He could take her in any direction now.

The van slowed and turned left. Was this their destination? The engine died. Everything was quiet. Suzie shouted for help at the top of her voice. She could hear nothing. The cloth bag was slowly suffocating her; she felt lethargic. Suzie willed the adrenaline needed to attack her captor when the time came. She had to throw off this stupor and find the courage to escape. To sit and wait for what he planned for her was not an option.

The van's rear doors opened, and the man removed the handcuff from the metal framework on the interior wall. He soon secured both of Suzie's wrists in front of her. He dragged her to the doorway. Suzie felt a warm breeze on her bare arms as she felt the edge of the van floor under her feet. She caught him unawares. Suzie ripped the bag off her head and, clasping her hands together, swung hard across the man's face as she sprang forward.

Suzie landed on her feet and stumbled but soon ran for her life.

At last, she could see the lay of the land. The van sat in front of a 1930s detached house. Mature trees screened the driveway from the road. She glanced left as she reached the pavement. Her captor was already in pursuit. Wherever she was, there were no other houses within a hundred yards in that direction. She had to go to her right. Suzie prayed they were on the outskirts of a small town. Surely she could outrun a guy twenty years her senior? She sprinted to her right, looking for signs of life, another property, and a vehicle to flag down. There had to be something. Where was everyone?

The man was closing. It was her fault. She was doing what every woman does when chased in a horror film. They trip and fall or run into a blind alley. Suzie knew that with each frantic attempt to locate an escape route, she slowed in anticipation of the need for a sudden change of direction.

The road surface was dreadful, with potholes everywhere. Suzie could feel the man's breath on her neck. Her right foot caught a hole's edge and turned her ankle. Pain screamed through her leg, and she sprawled forward onto the tarmac. The handcuffs prevented her from making a comfortable landing. Her arms were torn and bleeding after scraping along the rough surface.

The man jumped on top of her. Suzie screamed as his knee rammed into the small of her back. Two minutes, Suzie thought. He chased me for two minutes, and nobody saw or heard a thing. So much for her dash for freedom.

Suzie struggled in vain as her captor led her towards the house. The fall had winded her, and he was too strong. Her heart sank when she saw her purse, shopping bags and suitcase on the van's front seat. That explained the delay in leaving the car park.

Nothing remained to show anything untoward, let alone evidence of a kidnapping. Suzie's parking ticket expired after four hours. Someone would slip a note beneath a windscreen wiper to say she would receive a fine through the post. It could be ages before anyone thought to check for her car hidden away in Leamington Spa. The town had never been on her list of destinations. Without that tailback on the M5, she could have been safe at home in Worton.

Once inside the house, the man pushed her towards the first room off the hallway. It was small and dark. Everything smelled musty as if the house had been empty for ages. The door closed, and Suzie heard the snap of a padlock. She ran to the bay window, but a lock secured every exit point.

Suzie checked her surroundings. She had visited several similar properties in her time. This room was the sitting room that families kept for high days and holidays in the decade following the war. The dining room and kitchen lay at the back of the house, where the family spent most of their time. There was no central heating, but the kitchen was always warm.

Few homes had a television in those days, so everyone crowded around the radio in the dining room. The large table offered plenty of space for games of cards, board games and jigsaws. Suzie realised she was rambling. It was hard to concentrate.

Why was someone holding her prisoner, anyway? The man hadn't attempted to touch her. Thank God. He hadn't spoken one word to her throughout the ordeal. There had to be something she was missing.

Suzie listened for movement inside the house. Where was he? She hadn't heard the front door since they came indoors. Was she alone in the dark with nobody coming to rescue her? Suzie bit her bottom lip. She refused to cry. There was nothing to do but wait and worry about what followed. Suzie sank into the nearest comfortable chair.

It was morning when she awoke. Suzie blinked hard to clear her head. The events of yesterday afternoon came rushing back. Her elbows, forearms and knees stung from the cuts and scratches she had suffered. Her mouth was dry.

"Is there anyone there?" she croaked.

Suzie heard heavy footsteps on the stairs, and a kettle whistled behind her in the kitchen. She could hear a faint clicking of china and cutlery. Was this breakfast for one or two, Suzie wondered. The padlock scraped against the wooden door, and the man opened it just enough to slide in a tray. The door closed again, and the lock snapped shut at once.

"What do you want?" cried Suzie, "why are you keeping me here?"

There was no reply.

The breakfast tea was drinkable, and Suzie devoured the two slices of toasted white bread. She wouldn't recommend wearing handcuffs while breakfasting, but she coped. There was no cutlery. What an idiot to think he might have left a knife or spoon for her to unscrew the window locks. Suzie wondered what Gus was doing this Saturday morning. She missed him.

Stop thinking of Gus, she scolded herself. Don't get emotional. Keep learning what you can about the man who's taken you and where this house is. You have to believe that your parents will raise the alarm.

Suzie brushed her teeth with her finger. She needed to use the bathroom. She called out and sighed with relief when she heard the padlock opening. Her captor led her across the hallway to a downstairs cloakroom with no toilet paper. She longed to climb to the shower or bath she imagined was behind the door she could see at the top of the stairs.

He never offered her the chance to get washed. So far, the small front room with shuttered windows and the loo were the only rooms she could describe to her colleagues.

If she ever got out of here alive.

There was nothing in either room to show who lived there. The décor was dated, and the furniture was sparse but functional. Perhaps that was why the man brought her here. It might have been his parent's home, even if the shiny stainless steel padlock was a recent addition.

To pass the hours until the next visit from her captor, Suzie imagined what lay behind the wall. Did they have comfortable chairs next door and dining chairs? Were there French windows leading into the garden? Could you access a conservatory from the kitchen? How many bedrooms were upstairs? She thought it was three rather than two. Did her captor have a brother or sister? What was it like growing up here?

In his formative years, what turned him into a predator who collected women off the streets and imprisoned them? Suzie was determined not to think of herself as a victim. She was a survivor.

Chapter Two

Monday, 21 May 2018

NEIL DAVIS WAS first in the Crime Review team office and was glad to be back. His father's death was still fresh in his mind, but now Neil knew the name of Terry's killer. Gus Freeman would make sure Ricky Gardiner paid in full for his crime.

Neil looked up to see Gus walking from the lift.

"Morning, guv," said Neil, "are you OK?"

"Hardly, Neil. John Ferris rang me just as I was leaving home. DI Ferris attended a digital and cyber-crime course for the last ten days. Her parents expected her home on Friday. Suzie spent the previous weekend in the Midlands, so it was always possible she would stay there longer. John said they began to wonder when Suzie didn't get in touch by last night, and he phoned her. There was no response."

Alex Hardy, Luke Sherman and Lydia Logan Barre arrived together and caught the end of the conversation.

"Who's missing, guv?" asked Alex.

"Suzie Ferris," said Gus, "I'm heading straight to London Road for a meeting on our last case, but this matter will get priority."

"What can we be getting on with while you're gone, guv?" asked Alex.

"Alex, you can ensure everything we uncovered on the McGuire case gets included in the Freeman Files. Lydia, clear the decks ready for action. Despite everything that's blown up in our faces this morning, I expect to bring another cold case back for us to unravel. Luke, your stint ends with us on Friday. Perhaps you could help Neil with what he's doing."

"Do I need to get him to sign the Official Secrets Act, guv?" asked Neil.

Neil was hunting details of the other course members when Dominic Culverhouse and Sandra Plunkett attended the old Bramshill House Training College together. A young man died in a hit-and-run accident late one night six years ago. Gus Freeman believed those two were attempting to cover up their involvement in his death.

"Not on this occasion, Neil, but that task *is* confidential, Luke. For our eyes only. Do you understand?"

"I get it, guv. You can rely on me."

Gus hurried to the lift.

"Right then, Luke," said Neil, "the hunt begins. We need the names and addresses of those officers on the same course in 2012. We're looking for hotels in the Basingstoke area that the various police forces used to house those senior officers during their stay. Gus wants to interview as many people as possible to confirm the events leading to the hit-and-run accident on the B3400 Andover Road. Jason Whitworth was cycling home after work on the twenty-second of September when a car struck him from behind. The following morning, a passing motorist spotted his body and broken bicycle in the ditch.

"Nasty," said Luke, "and they never found the driver?"

"No, but once we've found the other police officers in the area, our next task will be to locate the car involved."

"That might be difficult," said Luke, "unless they found evidence from the car at the scene."

"Oh, we don't need that," said Neil, "Gus knows who the driver was, so we need to check which car he drove at the time."

Luke looked puzzled.

"I know, mate," said Neil, "now you can see why it's confidential."

Luke started whistling. ♫ There could be trouble ahead♫.

Alex and Lydia shared a glance. Luke was a round peg in a round hole. What a shame he had to return to his old job.

GUS DASHED into Reception at London Road. Before John Ferris's call, his original plan was to sign in, get upstairs to see the ACC and collect the murder file for his next case. Gus planned to stall the ACC on the McGuire business and hoped to get away with promising to have the data with him later today. However, the call meant that a search for Suzie needed to begin as soon as possible. What lay behind her uncharacteristic disappearance?

The young officer at Reception was speaking to him, but his thoughts were on Suzie. Gus realised the lad was holding a phone towards him. He grabbed it impatiently and answered.

Gus stopped breathing as he heard the sinister voice.

"Suzie Ferris dies if you open your mouth."

Ricky Gardiner rang off before Gus could reply. Gus reached the top of the stairs and found DS Geoff Mercer smiling at him without a care in the world. Gus blanked out the small talk. He was thinking about Gardiner and why he had taken Suzie.

Geoff finished speaking and tapped on the ACC's door. Gus followed his friend inside the office. The ACC looked in better form than before his few days' holiday.

There was no preliminary chat this morning. It was straight to business.

The ACC's first request was for an update on the McGuire case. Gus decided to wing it. He admitted the investigation was going nowhere. He suggested sticking the file back in the box until someone else had nothing better to do. Gus expected a chilly reaction to that news.

Gus reckoned if they pursued Ian McGuire's killer and the case reached the courts, it would create a bigger mess than if they drew a veil over it here and now. Kenneth Truelove prattled on about the Chief Constable not liking that Gus now had something in the Loss column after three straight Wins.

The three men knew Dominic Culverhouse and Sandra Plunkett wanted the Crime Review Team out of business. They'd known that before Terry Davis ventured home from Marbella for the first time in five years. What hadn't been clear was how far the duo would go to protect the secret Terry held.

They had paid Ricky Gardiner to keep tabs on Gus and his activities. Who knows how many of his friends and colleagues were under surveillance? Gus could only speculate on what they planned to do. However, Terry's arrival in Devizes increased the pace and scale of things altogether.

Culverhouse and Plunkett panicked and ordered Gardiner to remove the perceived threat posed by Terry Davis.

Last week, besides attending to the McGuire cold case review, Gus secured extra resources to investigate Terry Davis's murder. They now knew Gardiner was their man. On Friday, when Suzie was supposed to be driving home from the Midlands, Neil gathered the final pieces of the Bramshill and Oakley jigsaw. Gus shared none of that information with Geoff and the ACC last week.

Was there nothing he could do without the Chief Constable and her cronies hearing about it? Who could have known how far his team had reached?

Gus was ticking names off the list in his head.

He believed it was time to show his hand.

"Until a few minutes ago, I was ready to tell you to charge Ricky Gardiner with Terry Davis's murder and start proceedings against Her Ladyship and Dominic Culverhouse. Neil has a few hours of work to do chasing evidence and getting witness statements, and we will be ready to go ahead."

"What's changed?" asked Geoff Mercer.

"Gardiner has kidnapped Suzie Ferris and threatened to kill her if we use everything we know against them."

"What?" said Geoff Mercer, "I hadn't seen Suzie this morning, but I had no idea she was missing. What on earth happened?"

Gus explained the phone call from John Ferris. Failing to contact her parents was out of character. Whatever caused her to change her plans to return home on Friday afternoon meant Suzie had been missing for sixty hours. However, the phone call from Gardiner just before Gus came upstairs solved one problem. They now knew Suzie had been taken against her will by a known killer.

"I don't like the sound of that one bit," said the ACC.

"Don't lose your nerve now, Sir," said Geoff Mercer.

"I don't intend to, Mercer," said the ACC, "modern policing shouldn't be represented this way. These people are worse than criminals. They're supposed to be setting an example. Right, Freeman, what can we do to help?"

"I want to keep DS Luke Sherman on the team for the time being, Sir. The sooner we can close the net on Culverhouse and Plunkett, the better, regardless of the threat Gardiner issued."

"He killed Terry Davis," said Geoff, "We can't risk him getting a taste for it. I'll call his handlers in the Met to check whether he has a history of excessive force in any other cases. I can't allow DI Ferris to get sacrificed. Even if saving her derails our attempt to bring down two corrupt high-flying officers."

"I'll hold the fort here, Mercer," said the ACC, "you get over to the CRT office. Grab the young WPC you borrowed last week. She acquitted herself well. I'll square it with her, Sergeant; he owes me a favour. We must keep a lid on what we're doing, loose lips and all that. Her Ladyship won't hear a peep from me, and unless she visits the CRT office, she won't know who's working there and on what. Your office is on the first floor, Freeman. The only access is by lift, yes? Don't bloody let her inside the office. Is that understood?"

"Yes, Sir," said Gus.

"Start the lads in the Hub on a search for Ferris's car. Concentrate on the area between the College for Policing and her most likely route home. Does she have a GPS tracker on her vehicle? What about her mobile phone?"

"I don't know the answer to the first question, but her father told me her mobile is unresponsive Sir," said Gus.

"That's unusual, isn't it? Ferris and others like her

carry a charger with them wherever they go. They run their lives through a blessed smartphone. If she was at Ryton-on-Dunsmore for ten days, it needed regular recharging. Who was on the same course? Identify them, and discover the last person to see her. Which way did she travel home? Let me think. Credit card, yes, check for that too. A modern girl, like Ferris, probably uses this tap-and-go business and never needs to scrabble through her pockets for loose change. If there's anything else that narrows the field for her whereabouts, add them to the list."

"I think that's enough to be going on with, Sir," said Geoff Mercer.

"One thing, Freeman, before you dash off," said the ACC.

"Yes, Sir?"

"What was it you discovered in the past couple of days you intended to enlighten us with this morning?"

"Culverhouse and the Chief Constable attended a course at Bramshill in 2012. A twenty-six-year-old cyclist from Basingstoke died in a hit-and-run. Nobody found the body until the following morning, and they never traced the driver."

"You're sure one of our mutual friends hit him? I assume the other person was in the car at the time?"

"Yes, Sir. Terry Davis discovered the truth and believed it was one of his 'get out of jail free' cards. But, unfortunately, they couldn't risk Terry letting me in on the secret, so Gardiner silenced him."

"How did you learn of their involvement if Davis hadn't told you yet?" asked the ACC.

"Terry left a cryptic clue with Donna, one of his confidential informants. He passed it to her in a pub he visited on Sunday night. A little detective work unlocked the clue, and now we need to fill in the finer details."

"When will I receive the files on the McGuire case? I hoped you would nail someone for that. I wanted to keep the Chief Constable off our backs, not just because I wanted Tony Brown to learn we'd caught the killer. It played on his mind, you know, he put everything into that case and got nowhere. He was never the same man after that."

"You'll have the files by this afternoon, Sir," said Gus, "You'll see that we did our best. Someone much cleverer than me said you can't win them all."

"That chap Kierkegaard again, I bet," said the ACC, "I can't say I've ever read any of his books. I sense his philosophy wouldn't fit with my religious beliefs. You set great store by him. Each to his own."

"I believe it was Connie Mack, an American businessman who said you can't win them all," said Gus, "but don't quote me on that."

"Another wise man said that," said Geoff Mercer, "time we left."

Geoff and Gus left the ACC in his chair.

"That's the most I've heard him say since I've known him," said Geoff.

"He was on the money with his list of priorities, Geoff. It's a pity he's retiring a year from now. We could make a decent copper out of him, given time."

"Kenneth's always been one of the good guys," said Geoff, "sometimes, a promotion takes an officer out of the action too soon. The ACC got the job done when he was an Inspector. His uniformed officers spoke highly of him; I can guarantee that. He loved being in the thick of it. Once he made ACC, the job became meetings, budgets, targets and initiatives. He can cope with anything anyone throws at him, but times like this are his forte. Although, like us, he'd rather not have to face up to one of our female officers getting kidnapped."

"I'll drive to the CRT office," said Gus, "and inform Luke Sherman that he's staying. I'll brief the team on what's required."

"Thanks. My first task is to round up WPC Cranston, and then I'll visit the Hub to set the wheels in motion there. Amelia and I should be with you in an hour."

"Fair enough," said Gus, "see you later."

Gus sensed movement to his right. It was Vera.

"How much can you tell me?" she asked.

"What have you heard?" asked Gus.

"Suzie's not returned to work as planned. We've received no phone call to say she's ill. You and Geoff Mercer seem stressed. Are the two related?"

"Try not to worry," said Gus, "we're on top of things. I can't say more at present. Keep the ACC calm if you can. This morning, he might need a drop of Scotch in his cup of tea."

"Keep us in the loop, Gus," said Vera.

"You can count on it," said Gus. He pushed through the main door and made for his trusty Ford Focus. What a start to the week.

WHEN HE REACHED the Old Police Station, Gus found the team engrossed in their tasks. That was a relief. The rumour mill hadn't started its work yet. He needed them to focus on the priorities today. They couldn't afford to get embroiled in a pity party for Suzie Ferris. He worried enough for everyone already.

"What's the latest, guv," asked Alex.

"Give me a chance to get my feet under the table," chided Gus, "I'll bring you up to speed as soon as I can."

"Sorry, guv," said Alex.

"Let's get a few bits of admin out of the way before we tackle the meaty stuff," said Gus, "Neil, do you know when your father's funeral is yet?"

"Thursday week, guv, on the thirty-first. It's the same venue as Frank North. I assume you'll travel over to West Wilts Crematorium together. The service is at ten-thirty in the morning this time."

"We'll be there," said Gus, "variety is the spice of life, they say, but I've had my fill of funerals."

"You've got Tony Brown's to attend yet, guv," said Alex.

"Exactly, Alex," said Gus, "Luke, your stint with us will continue. I hope you don't object?"

"Not me, guv. While doing this, I'm not doing something I dislike."

"When this latest crisis is over, I suggest the team gets together for a drink one Friday night to show how much we've appreciated you filling the gap."

"You'll get no complaints from us, guv," said Lydia, "we haven't had a team night out for a while."

"We didn't have cause to celebrate on the last case," Alex reminded her. "Despite the many hours we put in, it wasn't possible to bring Ian McGuire's murderer to justice."

Gus stepped through every element of the McGuire case in his head for the umpteenth time. He prayed nobody spotted the potential killer in the Freeman Files among the names of those they interviewed or their relatives.

"We have two extra pairs of hands joining us in the next thirty minutes," Gus continued. "DS Mercer and WPC Cranston will help us co-ordinate the search for DI Ferris.

The ACC approved the added resources so Neil and Luke can concentrate on tying up loose ends on the case they're pursuing."

"Amelia's a bright girl," said Neil. "she'll be an asset in more ways than one."

"You're married, Neil," said Lydia, "you aren't supposed to notice. Especially with Melody three months gone."

"I can look," said Neil, "that's still legal. You're single, Luke. You could ask Amelia to the team get-together once we're out of this chaos."

"What makes you think I haven't got someone to bring, anyway?" asked Luke.

"Do tell," said Lydia.

"That's enough," said Gus, "there will be time for light-hearted banter later. DS Mercer has asked the Hub people to start the search for Suzie's Volkswagen Golf GTI. I need you and Alex to concentrate on identifying who was on the same digital and cyber-crime course. Who was the last person to see her? Where was Suzie heading when she left Ryton-on-Dunsmore? Alex will know the questions we need to answer. Where has he gone?"

"He went to the restroom, guv," said Neil, "it must be time for his pills."

"I had to remind him last week not to overdo things," said Gus. "He needs to give his mind and body time to heal. You can't rush these things. Alex risks doing more damage."

The lift doors opened, and Geoff Mercer entered the CRT office with Amelia Cranston.

"Good morning, everyone," said Geoff, "I wish I could visit the CRT on a more pleasant occasion. WPC Cranston and I are pitching in to help locate DI Ferris and return her to her family safe and well."

"Is DI Ferris in danger, Sir?" asked Neil. "We heard she was missing, but there can be several innocent reasons for that."

Gus and Geoff shared a glance. Gus nodded.

"This is not a run-of-the-mill missing person case, DS Davis. DI Ferris disappeared after one o'clock on Friday afternoon. Her current whereabouts and condition are unknown. As soon as Gus stepped inside the door at London Road earlier this morning, he received a phone call. It was from a man who said he had Suzie Ferris and threatened to kill her."

Lydia gasped.

"My God, how dreadful. Why would he want to kill her?"

"Is this related to Neil's father's death?" asked Alex, who was returning to his desk.

"It's complicated," said Gus. "Last week, you, Lydia, and I concentrated on the McGuire case. Luke split his time between that investigation and helping Neil. As you know, Neil and Amelia went through hours of CCTV footage searching for Terry Davis's killer."

Alex glanced across at Luke and Lydia. They hadn't picked up on the relevance of that exchange. He'd queried why a senior officer such as DS Mercer was checking CCTV footage last Wednesday. It was only on Thursday that Amelia Cranston arrived to help Neil.

He thought it was odd behaviour at the time. It made less sense now.

"Neil asked whether Luke should sign the Official Secrets Act earlier, guv," said Alex. He dived in headfirst. "The matter that Luke and Neil are working on is confidential. Wouldn't it be simpler to let us know what's happening? It's plain that DS Mercer is leaving out important bits of information. Sorry, Sir, if I'm speaking out of turn. But was it the same man you believe murdered Terry Davis who has now taken DI Ferris? If so, who is he?"

"We're trying to protect you, Alex," said Gus, "as I said, it's complicated."

"Neil and Luke are already involved, guv," said Lydia. "if ramifications follow their investigation, then the Crime Review Team will suffer. You'll go back to your gardening, and Alex and I will get reassigned to other teams. Heaven knows what will happen to Neil and Luke. We can only survive as a team if we stick together. Or am I being naïve again?"

"Far from it, Ms Barre," said DS Mercer, "you and DS Hardy have just shown why I believed you were the best people to form this team. I can't divulge everything, but this goes deeper than you can imagine. As for you, WPC Cranston, your career is in its infancy, and if you wish to return to London Road, I'll take you back there now. Gus Freeman can put the rest of the team in the picture while I'm gone. Let me warn each of you. There's no turning back once we start on this path."

"Death or glory, Sir," said Neil, "I owe it to my father to see this through to the end."

"It sounds more exciting than what I've done so far, Sir," said Amelia, "if it doesn't work out, I'm young. I'll find another use for my talents."

Neil coughed. Lydia gave him the stare.

"I hope you don't regret it," said Geoff Mercer. "When we studied CCTV records in the Devizes centre on Wednesday, Gus Freeman and I traced a man tailing Terry Davis as he visited several bars on Sunday evening. We confirmed his identity on Thursday with the help of Neil and Amelia. His name is Ricky Gardiner, and he started as a beat copper in the Metropolitan Police in the mid-Eighties. He spent more than half his career undercover. His handlers lost track of him on more than one occasion. They were never certain whose side he was on. I checked his record after Gus left London Road this morning. Gardiner earned a reputation as an enforcer. There were so many red flags against him when he quit; they could have made a quilt. Once on the outside, Gardiner started offering his skill set to the highest bidder. On that Sunday night, eight days ago, Gardiner killed Terry Davis."

"Who wanted Terry Davis dead?" asked Alex.

"That's as far as I'm prepared to go," said Geoff. "Until Suzie successfully reunites with her family and Gardiner is in custody, Neil and Luke will carry on with the assigned tasks. Then, we will move heaven and earth to find where Gardiner has taken Suzie Ferris. I can reveal the bigger picture once we're successful."

"Who's doing which task?" asked Gus.

"Amelia can liaise with the Hub. They're searching for Suzie's car. That's our starting point."

"What year is it?" asked Amelia.

"Last year's model," said Geoff.

"She could have the location-sharing application that VW made available in 2015. My Dad wanted it fitted on my car. You can let a friend or family member know your arrival time. Businesses can inform customers when a service technician will arrive at their house. The app lets you share your location with anyone you nominate for as long as you wish."

"There's a timer for location sharing, though, isn't there?" asked Lydia, "I believe it lasts for four hours. Once your selected time runs out, your location will no longer be shared."

"I'll ask John Ferris whether Suzie got it fitted," said Gus, "either way, excellent thinking. Keep the ideas flowing, all of you."

Gus watched as the room sprang into life. The mood felt different. When Geoff Mercer brought him here for the first time only seven short weeks ago, it was in preparation for a team of four. For the next few days, their number had swelled to seven.

Gus hoped it retained its reputation as a lucky number. He turned to Geoff Mercer, who was sharing his desk.

"When I call John Ferris, I'll ask about Suzie's phone. They knew she had made plans to spend the middle weekend in the Midlands. Was that the last contact they had?"

"Good idea," said Geoff, "I'm getting in touch with the College for Policing. The ACC may have notified them that DI Ferris is missing. We need their co-operation in providing the names of those officers they had with them last week."

"What have you got Alex and Lydia doing?" asked Gus.

"I asked them to dig into Ricky Gardiner's background. Thanks to Neil and Amelia, we have an excellent recent photo of him. With the Hub's help, we can search for him on CCTV in the vicinity of the College on Friday. We know how he moved around while stalking you in the village, but he must have used a vehicle on this occasion. It would help if we knew the make and model. Oh, ask John Ferris for her bank and card providers. How does she pay for goods and services? That's the other avenue Alex and Lydia can follow while they await the Hub's search routine results."

Gus picked up the phone to call John Ferris.

"Hang on, Gus. I think you should visit him in person. He thinks his daughter's missing. We know now this was a kidnapping. We must disclose that information."

"They're feeling lousy now. God knows what this will do to them," said Gus, "can I grab Lydia, please? We don't want me doing something without a chaperone to give the Chief Constable more ammunition to bury us."

"Fair comment," said Geoff. Gus made the call.

"John, it's Gus Freeman."

"Any news, Gus?"

"Nothing to pass on yet, John. We've got the whole team working on this now. I need a few pieces of information from you."

"Go ahead, ask anything you wish. Jackie's lying down at present. It's hit her hard. She can't understand why Suzie didn't get in touch. She's such a considerate daughter; never caused us sleepless nights."

"If you can stay where you are, John, I'll be over to see you in the next twenty minutes."

Geoff Mercer had asked Lydia to get ready to leave. Gus grabbed his keys, and they made for the lift.

"Do you want me to drive, guv," asked Lydia.

"I know where we're going," said Gus.

"Oh, you've been there before then," said Lydia.

"Read nothing into that, young lady," said Gus, "Suzie's father offered me a place of refuge after the shooting. I reached the farm on horseback to lie low for half a day. I arrived at my bungalow in a CSI van later that evening, thank goodness."

"You're not the horsey type then, unlike Suzie Ferris?"

Gus was glad of the chat, and it stopped him from fretting over Suzie's situation for a few precious minutes. Then, as he drove up the approach road to the farm, Lydia whistled her appreciation.

"Blimey, it's impressive, isn't it, guv? The farmhouse is

miles from the main road. At least they never get troubled with surprise guests."

John Ferris stood waiting by the door as Gus parked his Ford Focus in front of the farmhouse.

"Come on in," said John. He led them through the house and into the largest kitchen Lydia had ever seen.

"John, my colleague here is Lydia Logan Barre. She's a member of the Crime Review Team working on your daughter's case."

"You're classing it as a case, Gus? What does that mean?"

"Take a seat, John," said Gus. "Not long after we first spoke this morning, we learned that Suzie got kidnapped on Friday afternoon."

"Kidnapped, but why? Who would want to kidnap her? If there's a ransom, we'll pay it, no matter how much they're demanding."

"There was no mention of a ransom, John."

"So, it's personal, nothing to do with someone targeting us for financial gain?"

"We know who took her, John,"

"Ah, it was that Tim Yarwood, I suppose. They broke up within weeks of getting together again. I couldn't get my head around that. Suzie didn't go into details, but I'm surprised he would go to such lengths."

"It wasn't Tim Yarwood, John. Look, let's concentrate on getting her back. When was the last time you heard from Suzie?"

"The Friday before last, early in the evening. My wife, Jackie, told me Suzie called to say there was so much going on that it was a great chance to stay up there to relax and have fun."

"Was that call made to your landline?" asked Gus.

"Um, no, Suzie knows we're more likely to be somewhere on the farm at that time of day. She calls us on our mobiles."

"Did Suzie take her charger with her? I tried contacting her midweek and got no reply, but I left a message. She never answered, and now you say the phone's unresponsive."

"Whoever has her must have disabled the phone or destroyed it." Lydia saw John Ferris's shoulders sag. The seriousness of the situation was hitting home.

Gus realised someone was standing in the doorway, listening to their conversation.

"Jackie," said John Ferris, "come and sit by me, love. We've heard some news."

"Someone is holding our Suzie," said Jackie Ferris, "I heard you talking. I'd walked across to Suzie's room and lay on her bed. She sleeps above this kitchen. It's the first time I've been there uninvited since she was fifteen."

Jackie Ferris took a mobile phone out of her dressing gown pocket.

"This is Suzie's mobile. The battery must have been flat for ages—everything's upstairs, her charger, tablet, and laptop. I don't know why she didn't take any of it with her. No wonder we couldn't get in touch."

"Do you have your mobile, Jackie," asked Gus.

Jackie disappeared, then returned with her phone.

"The last call you received from Suzie, what was the number?" asked Gus.

Jackie read it out. Lydia made a note of it, then went outside to make a call.

"Is Suzie in danger, Gus?" Jackie asked. "Don't sugarcoat it. Tell us everything."

"Her kidnapper made a threat; I can divulge that much.

Its purpose was to force the police to abandon an ongoing criminal investigation. If we agree to his demands, then Suzie will come to no harm."

"Suzie's call came from the Ibis Hotel, guv," said Lydia, re-entering the kitchen, "only a short drive from the College.

"Call Alex," said Gus, "tell him where to start the search for our man. He must have carried out surveillance before Friday. See if they can identify the vehicle. A number plate would be a bonus."

"On it, guv," said Lydia.

"Can you get this investigation stopped?" asked John.

"It's a whisker away from completion," said Gus, "my focus is on getting Suzie home. There will be plenty of time to put the finishing touches to our case once we've removed the threat—one other thing I need from you two. Suzie may have made purchases while she was away. Did she use cash or a card?"

"Suzie always used her card for items over ten pounds," said Jackie, "I doubt if she carried more than twenty pounds in her purse."

"If you let me have her details, Jackie, then we can get our experts to get a list of what she spent and where and when she spent it. That will narrow the search for the crime scene."

Jackie walked through the hallway and disappeared upstairs.

"Is that it?" asked John.

"Does Suzie have a location tracking device on her GTI?" asked Gus.

John Ferris shook his head.

"I've no idea. If it came as standard, it's in there, but I wouldn't know what it looked like or how it works."

"Okay, John," said Gus. They had to locate the car another way.

Lydia was back from making her call. She gave Gus a thumbs-up.

Jackie returned soon after and handed Gus details of every card Suzie might be carrying.

"You know how much Suzie means to us, Gus," said Jackie, "she thinks a lot of you from what I've seen. We just want her home."

Jackie's voice broke as she spoke the last words. John moved across the kitchen to put his arm around her shoulder.

"I don't much care what happens to the bloke responsible," said John, "as long as we see our daughter walk in that door safe and sound."

"That's what we all want," said Gus.

Chapter Three

"A PITY ABOUT THE LOCATION TRACKING," said Lydia, "but you got everything else you wanted, didn't you?"

"We need as many tools as possible at our disposal, Lydia. Speed is of the essence. Gardiner issued his threat this morning. I don't believe he's received an instruction to kill Suzie yet. The people he works for will want to learn what progress we've made in tying the loose ends in the case against them before they act. We must ensure they don't find out we're pursuing those loose ends and hunting for Suzie and Gardiner."

"We don't have a mole in the Crime Review Team office, do we, guv?"

Gus knew it was unwise to assume anything.

"I sincerely hope not, Lydia. That's why speed is important. We need to neutralise the only weapon these people have. If we can locate and capture Gardiner, he can't harm Suzie. To achieve that, we need to solve our side of the equation quicker than the side Neil and Luke are tackling. Get it?"

Lydia got it. Gus drove them back to the Old Police Station.

WHILE THEY WERE IN WORTON, Geoff and Amelia were getting frustrated. They were waiting on data from the Hub relating to Suzie's car.

Alex made the most progress as he compiled a visible biography for Ricky Gardiner. He spotted a potential clue as he loaded the information onto the wallboard. He kept going. Alex glanced at his watch. Almost four o'clock. Gus should return soon. He would want all the possibilities at his fingertips. It was foolish to grab the first clue and ignore the correct answer hidden in the discard pile.

When Gus and Lydia arrived upstairs, Geoff Mercer walked over to meet them.

"I think I'll run Amelia home, Gus. We're not getting data from the Hub until the morning, so our progress will falter this afternoon. They promised it would be with us first thing. We'll make an early start. I'll collect Amelia at six. How were John and Jackie?"

"Jackie's struggling. John Ferris is a robust character. He'll stay strong and get her through it. We drew a blank on the GTI, so you must chase that via traffic cameras. Lydia has the bank card details. Regardless of whether the Hub's swamped with requests, I'll pester them for a breakdown of her spending. You might need to call the ACC and ask him to get the Hub to live up to the stellar reputation he keeps trumpeting."

"I'll drop into London Road after I've dropped Amelia at home."

"There was one odd thing that Jackie raised. Suzie didn't take her mobile with her. Her tablet and laptop were still at home. Suzie's phone probably died two days after she left home for the course."

"That seems crazy," said Geoff.

Geoff Mercer beckoned to Amelia Cranston. The WPC hurried across the room.

"Are you any good at getting out of bed early, Amelia," said Geoff.

"Only to go home, Sir," she replied with a grin.

The youth of today, thought Gus.

"I've almost finished this board, guv," said Alex, "do you want to look?"

"I've passed the request on to the Hub, guv," said Lydia, "what can I do to help?"

"Check through the Freeman Files one last time, Lydia, and then send the information to the ACC," said Alex, "we promised him the Files by this afternoon."

"We've got several balls in the air, Alex," sighed Gus, "well done for keeping on top of that job. It slipped my mind."

"Suzie Ferris is your priority, guv. That's understandable."

You don't know half of it, thought Gus.

Alex saw he was distracted and returned his attention to the wallboard.

There were more items to add. Gus would review its content in due course.

"I KNOW you can't go into much detail, Sir," said Amelia as Geoff eased his car into the start of the rush hour traffic. "But how prevalent is kidnapping in this day and age?"

"Kidnappings for ransom targeting high-net-worth individuals and middle-class citizens occur infrequently," replied

Geoff, "comparisons of country threat levels based purely on statistics are difficult. Most kidnappings in Europe link to feuds between organised crime gangs, which skews official statistics published by national authorities. Overall, there could be fifteen thousand offences a year."

"That's more than enough, Sir," said Amelia, "is it on the increase?"

"There's been a recent surge in the UK and France. Sometimes improved reporting procedures contribute to a significant increase in the total number of recorded incidents. The figures include a small percentage of kidnappings for ransom; the majority are abductions, cases of human trafficking and hostage-takings related to organised criminal gangs."

"This doesn't fall into those categories, does it?"

"That's very astute, young lady. Unfortunately, on rare occasions, a victim becomes a pawn the criminals use to influence a particular course of events."

"Like those US cop shows when the Mafia grab a witness's wife to prevent him from giving his testimony."

"Exactly, the victim is chosen because of how valued they are in the eyes of the witness."

"Suzie Ferris means a lot to the Wiltshire Police," said Amelia, "I wonder why this Gardiner fellow called Gus Freeman to relay the death threat?"

This morning, Geoff Mercer had wondered the same thing when Gus broke the news.

Gardiner might have asked the officer in Reception for someone senior, and Gus was first through the door. But, if he specifically chose Gus to deliver his message, Gardiner must know something he didn't.

"Gus was probably the first available detective," said Geoff, hoping to buy time.

"Gus Freeman is a consultant, Sir. He can't influence operational matters. Surely, you or the ACC should have been Gardiner's first choice?"

"Not sure it's important at this stage," said Geoff. "We received the threat, and the ACC and I were in the picture within minutes of the call. Our top priority has to be finding Suzie and getting her home."

"Have you handled a kidnapping case before, Sir? Is there a preferred method?

"I've been involved in very few, thank goodness. How you handle the case is different each time," said Geoff, "depending on who gets taken. Children are the worst. You must retain focus and not let your emotions run riot. You're no good to the victim if you're in a mess and can't think straight."

Geoff heard himself saying the words, but inside he was praying Suzie escaped. It might be her only hope. Gardiner and his employers always appeared to be one step ahead of the game. If they learned how close Neil and Luke were to tightening the noose, Suzie could become collateral damage. Gardiner would kill her, remove traces of his role in the conspiracy and then go into hiding.

He'd spent over twenty years learning the tricks of the trade. Every move the police made was from a playbook Gardiner helped to write. No wonder he spirited Suzie away with such ease. She stood no chance.

"Where do you want me to drop you, Amelia?" Geoff asked as they passed Wadworth's brewery.

"You wanted to go to London Road, Sir," she replied, "that suits me. My car's there."

"I'll pick you up at half-past five," said Geoff. "Don't worry. I have your address on file. Tomorrow, you can dispense with the uniform. You'll blend in better with the rest of the team."

"I don't think I've got clothes in my wardrobe to match Lydia Logan Barre," sighed Amelia, "she's stunning, isn't she?"

Geoff Mercer had to admit Amelia was right.

"I think the colour schemes are less garish now than when she first joined the CRT. Gus had a quiet word, but Lydia has a personality you can't tame. Gus favours the same approach that I follow when meeting the public. We don't want to scare them for one thing, and it pays to tone everything down when we deliver dreadful news. Of course, that applies to your language and your appearance."

Geoff pulled into the HQ car park and reversed into his parking space.

"That makes sense, Sir. I'll have an early night. See you at half-past five."

Amelia Cranston disappeared around the end of the building, heading for the central car park.

Geoff Mercer trotted up the steps to the front door and went inside. There was still plenty of activity in the building.

The admin staff were the only ones working regular hours. Vera and Kassie were on the first floor and had another thirty minutes before they left. Geoff knew he wouldn't make it to his office without interruption. So, he stopped by Vera's desk to save the hassle.

"How's Gus?" she asked.

"Is there any news on Suzie?" asked Kassie.

"Gus and the rest of the team are doing everything they can to find Suzie," said Geoff, "it's early days, and the Hub will give us a good many leads. I'm visiting them to bash a few heads together. The Hub staff need to raise their game. Time is against us."

"The ACC had a visit from the Chief Constable," said Vera, "I thought you should know."

"I'm not surprised," said Geoff, "is the ACC still here?" Vera nodded.

"I'll visit the Hub first," said Geoff. "Can you ask him to hang around until I get back? I want to update him on our progress."

"Leave it with me," said Vera. "Will Gus be home this evening?"

"I can't say when he'll finish, Vera. I'm sure he'd appreciate a friendly voice, though."

Geoff went to his office to check what additions to the force's caseload had come in during the day. His other DIs needed someone to liaise with over the next forty-eight hours if he committed his time to helping Gus. So he called Gareth Francis and asked if he thought he could step up and cover. Geoff knew the answer would be in the affirmative. Gareth could be a prat, but nobody could accuse him of lacking confidence in his ability.

Once Geoff felt happier, things wouldn't go pear-shaped while off-site, and he made his way to the Hub. His mission was to get every scrap of data Gus Freeman might need on his desk in the Old Police Station office before the sun came up in the morning.

When he returned to the admin area, Kassie and Vera had left for home. He was confident the information Gus was waiting for was available now. Geoff realised his chances of winning the Mr Popular contest this year took a sizeable dent with the Hub staff, but that was tough. Geoff had reminded them that failure to deliver could put a colleague's life in danger.

He knocked on the ACC's door and entered. The ACC sat in his chair with a cup of tea. Geoff spotted crumbs on an otherwise empty plate on his desk. Vera and Kassie had ensured a comfortable wait.

"Anything yet?" asked the ACC.

"No news is good news?" suggested Geoff.

"Her Ladyship was on the warpath," said the ACC. "She breezed through the door as soon as I received the McGuire case files. If we hadn't swept this room for bugs last week, I'd swear she knew they were here. I hadn't even opened the blessed file."

Geoff sat opposite the ACC. He'd asked the Hub for a device to check for bugs. Was it possible the office computers were the security issue? That was something to add to the tasks he needed to cover.

Did they have a hacker at work at London Road?

"What did Ms Plunkett have to say," he asked.

"She wasn't interested in the detail. She only wanted to hear the bottom line. Had the killer been identified? There was no choice but to admit Gus couldn't solve the riddle. I think that was the first smile I've ever seen from her. I pray I never live long enough to see another. Sinister doesn't express the half of it. I pretended to listen to her droning on about the waste of resources. She questioned the wisdom of bringing officers out of retirement and the wanton disregard of the chain of command. I think that last bit referred to Gus conducting informal interviews with Monty Jennings and Peter Morgan in this building."

"Morgan probably ran to Miss to complain," said Geoff.

"Did I forget anything when I made my suggestions on how to proceed earlier?

"No, Sir, it was comprehensive. We found Suzie's phone. She never took it with her. We don't understand why yet.

I'm hoping we'll make great strides in the morning. Everything hinges on the Hub coming up with the goods."

"That's what they're there for," said the ACC. "I think I'll finish this cuppa and get off home. Her Ladyship is still hanging around somewhere. Will Freeman make it home tonight, do you think?"

"I believe Vera is hoping he will. She plans to call later."

"Vera and Freeman make a good pair. They're both single now, of course. I think you and I understand how important a firm family base is in this job."

"Now that you mention it. I'd better get home to Christine. I need to tell her I'm leaving just after sunrise. Gus wants to make an early start."

"My good wife will leave for her Pilates session in ten minutes. My dinner will be in the oven, no doubt. Still, we'll have an hour together after she returns before we climb the wooden hill. Life's full of simple pleasures when you know where to look. eh, Mercer?"

"Quite right, Sir. I'll update you tomorrow. Perhaps we could meet at the same time?"

"Good idea," said the ACC, "if the smiling assassin has been to see me, I'll try to leave a note telling you where to search for the body."

Geoff left the ACC to savour the last drops of his cup of tea.

A search for the body. Geoff prayed it never came to that for any of them.

Tuesday, 22 May 2018

GUS LOOKED at his alarm clock. Was it six o'clock so soon?

Last night, he'd spent a couple of hours after Geoff and Amelia left sifting through the meagre information they had available. Geoff was right. They wouldn't achieve real progress until the Hub spewed out its reams of data this morning.

When he returned from visiting John and Jackie Ferris, Gus had noticed Alex looked drawn and tired. So he'd encouraged Alex and Lydia to head home, with instructions to get an early night and then join Geoff and Amelia on the early shift.

Gus ordered Neil and Luke to call it a day at seven o'clock.

"You look to be floundering, lads. Start again in the morning, fully refreshed."

He got no complaint from either man. They travelled in the lift together and went their separate ways.

Gus couldn't resist calling in to the allotment once he reached Urchfont. It was Monday evening, and Bert Penman and Clemency Bentham were hard at work, albeit at opposite ends of their patch of ground. Gus wondered whether this was by accident or design.

"Ah, Mr Freeman," said the Reverend, "and how are we this glorious evening?"

"I've had better days," said Gus, "we're dealing with a delicate and potentially dangerous case."

"Gosh. I won't pry. I hope everything works out for you."

"How are you two getting on?" Gus asked, with a nod in Bert's direction.

"Very well, considering," she grinned. "Bert stopped to pass on a few words of wisdom when he arrived, and then he moved as far away from me as possible to start work."

"I think you're growing on him," laughed Gus.

He spent fifteen minutes considering the progress of his plants, thinking of something unrelated to Suzie Ferris. But it was just what he needed.

Gus spotted Bert strolling towards him. The retired butcher stopped by Gus's teepee contraption for runner beans.

"I think your words of wisdom are required," called Clemency. "You should go to him."

"Are you two visiting the Lamb later?" asked Gus.

"I expect so, but not together. Were you thinking of joining one of us?"

"Time's against me, I'm afraid. I haven't eaten yet, and I have an early start tomorrow. Another time, maybe."

Gus joined Bert by the teepee and listened to the list of tasks that required his attention before the weekend.

"We have an urgent and troubling case, Bert...."

"Say no more, Mr Freeman. I'll handle it. You must turn your full attention to catching the villains."

It had been eight o'clock before Gus reached his bungalow. Then, not for the first time, he heard the phone ringing outside his home. The voicemail kicked in, and after he'd chosen a meal to nuke in the microwave, he replayed the message.

"Hi, Gus. It's Vera. We're all worried about Suzie. If you can give us any news, please call back. Miss you."

Gus considered whether to call. He had nothing new to tell Vera at this stage. Least said, soonest mended, Tess always said.

After the ' ding ', Gus retrieved the unappetising meal

from the microwave and washed it down with a cold beer. He went to bed early and slept in fits and starts. As usual, it was during the longest and deepest stretch of sleep that the alarm rang.

Gus showered and dressed and then opted for cereals and yoghurt for breakfast. It was far too early for a fry-up. He wanted to arrive at the CRT office before seven, if possible. As he drove through the village and eased into the main road to Devizes, he wondered why he didn't start work at seven every day. There was much less traffic.

Geoff and the others were in the swing of things already. It was clear the Hub had done the business. Gus had to decide where he wanted to stick his nose in first.

He didn't get a choice. Neil spotted his arrival and collared him straight away.

"We haven't had much luck with the attendees, guv," Neil said.

"We're two Detective Sergeants," added Luke, "and when we ask men and women way above our pay grade what they were doing on the night of Saturday the twenty-second of September 2012, their immediate response is, who wants to know?"

"I've uncovered Chief Constables, Commanders and ACC's at Bramshill House at the time, guv," said Neil. "I don't think the wall of silence is a sign they're complicit in the cover-up. As Luke says, we're working with one arm tied behind our back. If we worked with what they call the Independent Office for Police Conduct these days, they'd have no choice but to co-operate."

Gus suggested they concentrate on the hotels and the car.

"Do we have to enter our findings in the Freeman Files, guv?" asked Luke.

"Not on your life," said Neil, "this clandestine operation is unrelated to any cold case passed to us by the ACC."

"Definitely not," said Gus, "remember what Geoff Mercer said yesterday. There's no turning back. You should both record everything and store the paperwork in separate locations under lock and key. Computer files have a habit of getting wiped or edited. Your work must never fall into the wrong hands. One issue we have is that we aren't sure whose hands are safe."

"Does Gus suspect one of us?" Lydia asked Alex.

He looked up from the computer printout he was studying.

"Don't be daft. It's odds on to be another mole inside the London Road building."

"I've just remembered, guv," said Neil Davis, "you wanted to know the Chief Constable's partner's surname. It's Naomi Hall, and she's four years younger than Ms Plunkett. Her parents live in Oakley. Her father is an accountant, and her mother is a music teacher."

"Thanks, Neil," said Gus, "now get back to the hotels and the car."

Gus thought it was time to learn the sum of what they'd gathered so far from the data supplied by the Hub.

"Right, apart from Neil and Luke, can the rest of you shout out what you've gleaned from these print-outs? Who wants to go first? Amelia, what can you tell me about Suzie's car?"

"The list is comprehensive, Sir," she began. Gus realised the young WPC was nervous. Although she'd worked one-on-one with Neil last week, this could be her first time in the spotlight within a major case team.

"Let's concentrate on what you have from Thursday the seventeenth. Take your time. I know you need to use 'Sir' when you speak to DS Mercer, but it's not necessary for a mere consultant. I preferred 'guv' when I was a serving officer."

"OK, guv. Well, there's an image of Suzie's Golf GTI on the A45 at five-fifteen in the evening on Thursday. That ties in with her leaving the College of Policing to return to the Ibis Hotel."

"Isn't that the stretch of road with the busiest speed camera in the country?" asked Geoff Mercer.

"I believe so, Sir," said Amelia, "we next pick up her car arriving in the car park of the hotel. The time difference suggests she wasn't speeding."

"Does your image show other vehicles arriving then, Amelia?" asked Gus. "Can we check if Gardiner followed her on Thursday evening?"

"Hotel security cameras allow me to watch everything, guv. I could search for vehicles that appeared at times matching with Suzie leaving for the College or returning in the evening. We don't know what vehicle Gardiner used. He might have access to more than one."

"True," Gus admitted, "it would be too easy to spot a big black van following her everywhere she went."

"There *was* a black van behind her on the A45, guv," said Amelia, "but those images are snapshots, and the number plate isn't readable. When I view the car park film, I'll keep an eye open for black vans."

"That's sensible," said Gus, "but don't ignore other traffic entirely. That van driver could be anyone. An actual sighting of Gardiner is what we want. When's the next time the Hub caught Suzie's car?"

"That was on Friday morning, guv. The security camera at the Ibis shows her leaving the car park. Several cars followed her out at around eight-fifteen. I didn't spot a black van at that point. DI Ferris stopped for petrol at the Motor Fuel Group garage on the way to the College where she used pump number three and walked across the forecourt to the mini-supermarket to pay."

"I've got that card transaction here, guv," said Lydia, "time-stamped at eight thirty-eight. DI Ferris didn't add further purchases."

"When she returned to her car, there was an incident you might want to watch, guv," said Amelia. "The area around the pumps is under twenty-four-hour surveillance to catch any drivers making off without paying. One corner of the forecourt is shielded from the cameras by the large blue steel stillages you can see stacked on the right-hand side. As DI Ferris moves towards the exit, there's a van edging towards the other vehicles in the queue."

"It's your big, black van, Amelia, well spotted," said Geoff.

"But is it *the* big black van?" asked Gus, "go back a minute or two. When Suzie left the shop, the automatic doors closed behind her, and then they opened again. Hello, Ricky Gardiner; he was in the shop. Yes, I can see what you mean Amelia, he's quite aggressive in ensuring he doesn't leave too much of a gap between them. Right, can we see them after that?"

"The College of Policing has cameras, guv," said Amelia, bringing a new piece of action onto her screen.

"There's Suzie's GTI," said Gus, "she's out of the car and heading towards the main building. Why has she stopped? Who's that talking with her, I wonder?"

"I have the details of the course attendees," said Geoff, "there were half a dozen female officers around the same age as Suzie. Not sure who we have here, but she's a friend rather than a foe, I reckon, don't you, Gus?"

"We need to talk to her, that's definite."

"Did you see that, guv?" asked Lydia, "they both looked over their shoulder. Only for a second, but could they have heard something?"

"Or Suzie saw something and mentioned it to her colleague," said Alex.

"Can we see what's on that side of the car park?" asked Geoff.

"That camera concentrates on the main body of the car park close to the front of the building," said Amelia. "The one on the approach road completes the three-hundred-and-sixty degree picture but was out of action on the day."

"Why am I not surprised," said Gus, "Gardiner did his homework. He parked at the petrol station in the only dark spot and disabled the approach road camera allowing him to follow Suzie right up to the College front door."

"Geoff, can you identify that woman Suzie spoke to, please? Amelia, carry on tracking Suzie's movements. What time did she leave?"

"The course ended before noon, according to the staff at the College," said Geoff. "People spent time inside chatting over a coffee before they started to leave."

"I've got the footage cued up from ten past twelve, guv," said Amelia.

"Here come Suzie and that other woman again," said Geoff. "Suzie appears to be writing something in her notebook."

"A phone number, I bet," said Gus, "because Suzie didn't have her phone. Her friend does, did you see?"

"They say their goodbyes," said Amelia, "then they both leave the car park. There's a stream of cars leaving the site for the next five or six minutes. The black van's not among them."

"I've got the name of the officer we've just seen on the security camera," said Geoff, "she's DI Josie Bennett, based at Snow Hill. I'm ringing her now."

"Put her on speakerphone, Geoff," said Gus, "we can listen to what she has to say. Just concentrate on the fact Suzie's missing, don't go further at this stage."

The two-minute wait felt like a lifetime.

"DI Bennett, I'm Detective Superintendent Mercer from Wiltshire Police."

"How can I help, Sir?" Josie replied.

"We're concerned over the whereabouts of our colleague, DI Suzie Ferris."

"Suzie? I don't understand."

"When did you last speak to her?"

"Straight after the digital and cyber-crime course finished on Friday at the College for Policing, Sir. The last time we spoke was at around a quarter past twelve. We swapped phone numbers, talked about an ex-boyfriend, and then left for home. Why what's happened?"

"We don't know," said Geoff, "was anything troubling Suzie during her stay in the Midlands?"

"Suzie didn't have a care in the world until that last day," said Josie. "We had a blast when we socialised in the evenings and at the weekend. Everyone on the course stuck together. Of course, there was a mix of married and single people, but there weren't any fun and games if you know what I mean."

"I'm not interested in that," said Geoff, "you mentioned the last day? What happened on Friday?"

"Suzie said there was a bloke in the garage shop when she paid for her petrol. He had his back to her, but she didn't think she knew him. She reckoned the same chap drove a black van that followed her into the car park. Suzie asked if I'd seen it. I hadn't noticed him. Half a dozen male officers were crossing the car park. It was almost nine o'clock."

"What happened when you came outside again later?"

"Suzie was taking phone numbers. She didn't have hers with her."

"Did she say why?" asked Geoff.

"Her Chief Constable told her to leave any communication devices at home. She said they weren't required. Suzie didn't question it. Well, you don't, do you? I told her nobody else heard about leaving phones and stuff at home."

"Did you discuss anything else?" asked Geoff.

Gus swallowed hard.

"We were talking about marriage and kids. How difficult it can be to find Mr Right among your fellow coppers and the lowlifes you meet. She said she made the mistake of turning the clock back when an old boyfriend got in touch. It was a disaster. I asked Suzie for his number because a fit rugby player might suit my needs. Suzie promised to send it on once she retrieved her phone. She hadn't called. I thought she just forgot."

"That was when she left you, was it?" asked Geoff.

"Yeah, she got into her GTI and shot out of the car park."

"Did she say where she was heading?"

"The same as me, I guess, driving straight home, put the washing on, and get ready for the weekend."

"So, the last thing she said was to promise to forward this ex-boyfriend's phone number?"

There was a pause as Josie Bennett thought for a moment.

"She said something that didn't make much sense, now

you mention it. She told me to make sure I never forgot the guy's name."

Gus closed his eyes. That could have been worse.

"Do you mind telling me the reason for this call, Sir?" asked Josie, "is Suzie missing or in trouble? There's been no mention of any problems in our region."

"There may be a simple explanation, DI Bennett," said Geoff Mercer. "It's now Tuesday, and the last sighting we have for DI Ferris was the one you just described at lunchtime on Friday."

"I know people disguise their pain, and it comes as a terrible shock when they do something daft, but honestly, Sir, you're barking up the wrong tree if you think she was suicidal. No way was Suzie troubled in the way you're suggesting."

"I think we can agree on that, DI Bennett. Thanks for the information. I hope we can give you positive news soon."

Geoff ended the call and sat back in his chair.

"Now what?" he asked.

"We know Suzie was followed to the College grounds by Gardiner between half-eight and nine. She couldn't expect to recognise him, they'd never met, but she realised someone was trailing her. It was the Chief Constable who told Suzie to leave her phone at home."

"We only have Josie Bennett's word for that," said Alex.

Gus looked at him and wondered if he was on the same page.

"I think we can assume Josie wasn't lying," he muttered. "As for Her Ladyship, it fits the scenario she and Culverhouse prepared with Gardiner. Suzie was alone and in no position to call for help or let us know she was in danger."

"Where was Suzie's car spotted next, Amelia?" asked Geoff.

"Perhaps, I can save time, Sir," said Lydia, "the next credit card transaction was in Royal Leamington Spa. Suzie ate lunch in Prezzo in the Regent Court Shopping Centre."

"Which is the nearest car park?" asked Gus, jumping up from his chair.

"St Peters multi-storey, guv," replied Amelia, "that's close to both the major shopping centres."

"Suzie bought several other items in the next ninety minutes, guv," said Lydia.

"So, there's no record of her buying a ticket at this car park?" asked Gus.

"Jackie Ferris told us Suzie only used cash for small items, guv," said Lydia. "Perhaps she had enough pound coins in her purse to cover a couple of hours of retail therapy."

"Geoff, I need to get up to Leamington Spa to locate Suzie's car," said Gus.

"Not a chance, Gus. I have to go, and I should take someone with me," said Geoff. "Who's available?"

"Take Lydia," said Gus, "I guess we don't have more card transactions to track?"

"No, guv, Suzie bought shoes and underwear in Marks And Sparks, and that was it."

"So, she returned to the car park at around three? Does that tie in with the time-stamp on the transactions?"

"That makes sense, guv?" said Lydia.

She dropped her computer print-outs on Gus's desk and scurried after Geoff Mercer, who was holding the lift door open.

Gus watched the door close and offered up a prayer. He shook his head.

That's what came from spending too much time with Clemency Bentham.

Chapter Four

"WHERE ARE WE GOING?" asked Lydia as Geoff Mercer drove out of town towards Devizes. "Leamington's in the opposite direction."

"We have to do things by the book," said Geoff, "my first port of call is the Ferris farm. I want to pick up a spare set of keys to Suzie's GTI from John Ferris. We can't merely find the spot where Suzie parked her car on Friday afternoon, pick it up and drive it back. It's a crime scene. The keys will avoid breaking into the car and make it easier to get it back to Worton."

"If this Gardiner character is as devious you say he is, he won't have left fingerprints," said Lydia.

"Again, we can't assume anything," said Geoff. "The delay is a significant problem, I grant you, but if Suzie put up a fight, there may still be forensic evidence to gather. This car park comes under the Warwickshire Police banner. Before barging into their area, I need my ACC to warn them we're on our way. Keep your fingers crossed they're not under pressure. We need a Crime Scenes Investigation team to meet us. I'll defer to the locals on this one, and as long as the ACC plays his part, they'll let me do more than stand and watch."

"So, we're dropping by London Road, too?" asked Lydia, "I haven't been there since my interview."

"We were lucky you applied to join us, Lydia," said Geoff, "Gus speaks highly of you. He tries to hide his admiration of your abilities when we're speaking with the ACC."

"Why's that?" asked Lydia.

"He doesn't want to lose you, of course."

Lydia sat quietly beside Geoff for the rest of the journey. The lengthy drive from the road to the farm building was as impressive as it had been yesterday. Geoff left her in the car while he collected the spare keys. Ten minutes later, they parked in Geoff's space outside the London Road HQ.

"I won't be a minute," said Geoff, "we don't need everyone knowing our business. I need two minutes with the ACC, and then I'll be back."

When Geoff Mercer returned, Lydia could tell him nobody went in or came out while he was absent.

"You must be my lucky charm," he grinned. "We're good to go now. I've given the ACC something to occupy his mind. He'll have less time to fret."

"If anyone asks where you are, what will he say?" asked Lydia.

"I suggested he explains it away as a family emergency," replied Geoff. "It's not one I've used before to cover up a crafty holiday. People commiserate and move on when you mention an emergency; they're not keen on hearing the distressing details. It will be less likely to raise questions from the ACC's superiors."

"Does the ACC fret much?" asked Lydia as Geoff eased his Ford Kuga into traffic.

"Kenneth Truelove has his moments, but he's a solid, dependable copper. He's still capable of coming up with good ideas. I should have thought of it myself, but he's ringing Gus to ask him to call in and collect the next cold case murder file."

"I don't think it will please Gus when he hears that. He's got enough on his hands."

"True, but if Gus's team aren't working on a case that the ACC had on his schedule, then what are they doing?"

"Gotcha," said Lydia, "the Chief Constable could use it as a valid reason to close the Crime Review Team. I don't understand why she's got such a dislike for the work we're doing. But, it might become clearer when you unveil the big picture you mentioned."

"I can't expand on what you know already," said Geoff, "I suggest you sit back and relax for the next two hours. By the time we reach Royal Leamington Spa, the ACC should have cleared us to join the hunt for Suzie's car and the crime scene."

Lydia did as he suggested. While Geoff listened to his Abba Greatest Hits album that Christine bought him, Lydia caught up on sleep she'd lost last night.

"TODAY'S TUESDAY," Suzie Ferris told herself.

It was essential to keep track of the days. Suzie never wore a wristwatch, but despite the shuttered windows, it was possible to determine day from night. She had another clue. The breakfast service in her prison cell never changed. It was always tea and toast.

Suzie stared at the empty mug and plate on the floor by the door. Day four of the unbalanced diet. It was Tuesday, alright. At least her other meals showed variety. Either her captor couldn't or wouldn't cook for himself. He was fortunate that there was a wide range of takeaways in the vicinity.

The van was away from the house for thirty minutes to an hour each day. That was the time Suzie used on Saturday in a futile effort to break out of the room. On Sunday, she had broken every nail working on the window locks.

Yesterday, she yelled at him when he left her a chicken curry. It wasn't a complaint about the food or the solitary plastic spoon, but if he wouldn't let her shower or wash, then at least he could allow her a change of clothes. Suzie knew her belongings were sitting doing nothing in the house somewhere.

The man hadn't uttered a word since Friday afternoon. When she stopped yelling yesterday, he gave a brief dry laugh and ignored her pleas. It was times like that when Suzie felt her resistance crumble.

Who was he, and why had he taken her? How long was he prepared to keep her here in this house? When would her colleagues come to rescue her?

What was Gus doing at this very minute? Suzie realised she had no idea. Breakfast might be the same meal every day, but what if that day started at different times thanks to her kidnapper? Was it eight o'clock now, or noon?

Later, when she called out to say she needed the toilet, the man led her across the hallway. Suzie slowed to look out of the narrow window to the side of the solid oak front door. The sky was barely visible above a thick screen of trees on the edge of the property.

Suzie recognised it as another overcast morning or afternoon, and there was nothing to help her gauge the time of day. A firm shove in the back warned her to keep moving.

Her only consolation was that her captor closed the door while she was inside the toilet. The lock was broken, so he could open it whenever he wished. Suzie washed her hands in the small hand basin and wiped them on the curtains. When she came into the hallway, the strip of light from the window was no more. A piece of black cloth now covered the windowpane.

The door slammed behind her as she stomped into her cell, and the padlock snapped shut once again. Suzie sank into a chair and hugged her legs to her chest. Where are you, Gus? When will you come for me?

WHILE GEOFF and Lydia were travelling as quickly as possible via the M4 and M5 to reach Royal Leamington Spa, Gus Freeman was dashing towards London Road on what he considered was a complete waste of time. What conceivable reason could the ACC have to remove him from the hunt for Suzie Ferris? They were one step closer to finding her now they knew where Gardiner kidnapped her. The longer this went on, the more he worried over the possible outcome.

Gus rarely went a week without experiencing a niggle.

On Monday morning, the initial call from Gardiner was a shock to the system. He wasn't thinking straight that day. When he dropped by the allotment on his way home, the niggle that surfaced late in the afternoon vanished from memory. Gus chatted to Clemency and Bert on any matter unrelated to policing or Suzie Ferris.

Often, these meaningless conversations proved to be the ideal relaxation. When Gus's head hit the pillow, the niggle resurfaced and with it the answer to what was bothering him.

As he drove up Caen Hill, the latest niggle floated into his head. While waiting for the traffic lights to change near the brewery, he considered it and decided he didn't have the answer. Perhaps this trip wasn't a total waste. He could run his niggle past the ACC, and between them, they might solve it.

The London Road car park was busier than usual. Gus tried to avoid the place at this time of day if possible. The alarm that interrupted his sleep seemed so long ago now, and the day was catching up with him. He couldn't bother to hunt for a free space. He parked in Geoff Mercer's empty spot.

A glance at the ACC's window confirmed he was in his office awaiting his arrival. He must be alone. Fingers crossed, Ms Plunkett wasn't hovering inside the door to give him hell about the McGuire case.

Gus strode inside the building and signed in at Reception. The young officer was the one who handed him the phone yesterday morning.

"Did that man ask for me in person yesterday morning?" he asked.

The officer flicked back through the book on the counter.

"That call came in at nine fifty-eight, Mr Freeman. Yes. He asked for you by name."

"Can you tell me the number he used to call me?" asked Gus.

Even if he could, Gus thought it was a burner phone and of no use now.

"We have caller number display, Mr Freeman. I recorded it here in the log."

The young man turned the book around and pointed to the details beside the nine fifty-eight call record.

"Excellent," said Gus, noting the number. He ignored the name the caller supplied. It was Ricky Gardiner who rang, not a gentleman called Cliff Wall.

Gus took the stairs two at a time to the admin area. Vera and Kassie paused in their work, and he knew he would upset them by not stopping. The meeting with the ACC was too urgent. He smiled and rushed past them. The ACC's door was already open.

Gus walked inside, and Kenneth Truelove closed the door behind him.

"I thought I'd make sure Her Ladyship didn't catch your arrival," he said, "she was on the warpath yesterday. There's a major budgetary review meeting this morning, and she could be out of our hair until late afternoon. We must be thankful for small mercies. Even if the budgetary review results in further cutbacks."

"I was surprised you dragged me away from the office, Sir," said Gus, "the search for DI Ferris has to be more important than everything else, surely?"

"Yes, Freeman, of course, but I want the Chief Constable to believe things are progressing as normal. Out with the old, in with the new. When she asks why Mercer isn't at work, I'll say a family emergency called him away. I'll tell her we expect him back in a day or two. You know very well how she feels about you and the CRT. I want her to think you and the team are engaged in the early stages of your next case."

"Yes, I can see that makes sense," said Gus. "Do you have the murder file? I'll take it back with me, but heaven knows when we'll make a start."

The ACC handed over a thick folder.

"Here we are, not to be opened until you're free to give it your undivided attention."

"If I hadn't stopped at the traffic lights by the brewery on my way in, I would be out of the door now to help search for Suzie Ferris. However, something kept niggling away at the back of my mind. I welcome your thoughts."

"I will help in any way I can, Freeman."

"Right," said Gus, "Gardiner called me just before I came here for our ten o'clock meeting. That's fair enough. Ms Plunkett knows your schedule. Gardiner passed a message designed to make me think twice before filling you in on the gaps in our evidence against her and Culverhouse."

"It didn't have the desired effect, though, Freeman. We discussed everything we needed to complete the evidence gathering, plus the resources required to locate and release DI Ferris."

"That wasn't what caused the niggle, Sir," said Gus. "Suzie got kidnapped at three o'clock on Friday afternoon. Why not call me in the office or at home in the early evening? Why wait until Monday morning? What was the reason behind the delay of well over sixty hours?"

"I take it the answer didn't come to you between the brewery and London Road?" asked the ACC. "Forget it for now. Get back to the office, and good luck in the search for DI Ferris. Leave that problem with me. It will give me something to occupy my mind."

Gus thanked the ACC and left. It was lunchtime; Vera and Kassie were nowhere in sight. Gus was relieved and yet disappointed. He dashed downstairs and was soon in his car, heading back towards the Old Police Station office.

In his office, the ACC stood by the window, watching Freeman leave. Kenneth Truelove was pleased with his morning's contributions. Geoff Mercer was doing something useful in Leamington Spa, and if anyone asked where he was, he'd come up with a reasonable response. His ruse of passing Freeman the next cold case was a credible smokescreen to make the Chief Constable and Culverhouse think Freeman had abandoned the hunt for clues into events at Oakley.

There was only one problem left to solve.

As he watched Freeman's battered Ford Focus join the queue of traffic inching towards the centre of town, he analysed the question Gus posed.

Freeman said that Gardiner kidnapped DI Ferris at three o'clock on Friday afternoon. So why not call him in the office or at home in the early evening?

Unless someone at London Road leaked Freeman's office number or his ex-directory home number, Gardiner had no way to contact him. It made sense that the call came to this building, and it preceded their regular Monday meeting. That guaranteed Freeman would be there to take it. Also, the next two people he saw would be himself and DS Mercer.

The ACC realised that Culverhouse and Plunkett expected Freeman to say he was gaining crucial evidence relating to the events near Oakley in September 2012.

Perhaps they were still unaware he and Mercer were working with Freeman and that all three agreed to uncover the truth, regardless of the consequence? The ACC certainly hoped that was the case.

Kenneth Truelove glanced at the photograph of his wife on his desk. They had their ups and downs, but he wouldn't be without her. Retirement couldn't come soon enough. You can't beat the love of a good woman.

It was turning out to be a fruitful morning. He had the answer to Freeman's niggle because Gus was asking the wrong question. Not why was there a delay? Why was it DI

Ferris that Gardiner kidnapped? That was the question, and if you asked that first, then everything else fell into place.

The ACC checked his reasoning. Did Mercer realise the situation? How much did Vera know? Just when you thought things couldn't get any more challenging, circumstances proved you wrong yet again.

GEOFF AND LYDIA arrived in Leamington Spa at around the time Gus Freeman was flying down Caen Hill. As they approached the St Peter's car park, it was clear the ACC's phone call was a success. A white van stood half on the pavement and half on the roadway outside the main entrance. A Scenes of Crime Officer in his white protective clothing wandered inside to carry out his duties.

Lydia knew the sequence of events the various forensic personnel had to follow. Her tutor stressed the importance of getting every tiny detail right. A thirty-something sandy-haired man in a grey suit spotted their arrival. He waved a hand as he slipped on the natty overshoes.

Geoff walked across to make the introductions.

"I'm DS Mercer from Devizes," he said. "this is my colleague Lydia Logan Barre. You were expecting us."

"We were, Sir. My name is DI Andy Carlton. My DS is the Crime Scene Manager. Blessing Umeh, is already on the job. It's her first time, so be gentle with her. Although she won't thank you for it."

"We all have to start somewhere, Andy," said Geoff, "let's get inside and see what's what. Lydia, you'll find pairs of shoes in my boot."

Lydia soon found a pair to hand to Geoff Mercer. As she slipped a pair over her sensible flat shoes, she remembered the words of her tutor.

'We hold onto the disposable blue plastic shoe covers until the completion of a case, and the possibility of an appeal has ended. You need to secure and preserve the crime scene, keeping a record of everyone who enters and leaves.'

The crime scene tape was in place to keep the public away. Andy Carlton talked as he walked.

"We found the Golf GTI with no trouble. My grand-mother could have worked it out."

"I can imagine," said Geoff, "it was the only GTI in a space where the ticket was three days out of date. Apart from slapping a notice on the windscreen, did the car park people make any further enquiries?"

"Someone called us this morning. Cars get abandoned every day. Joyriders nick cars such as this GTI and then hammer around town until the early hours, causing mayhem. As often as not, they then set fire to them. People also dump them in a multi-storey rather than go through the rigmarole of scrapping them legitimately. We realised this didn't fall into either of those categories when we got the call from your ACC."

They climbed the stairs to the first floor. Lydia saw the cordoned-off area surrounding the GTI and the forensic staff hard at work.

DC Blessing Umeh stood to one side with a clipboard. She was concentrating so hard they were on top of her before she noticed their arrival. Lydia recognised the Nigerian Igbo surname. Lydia wondered whether her birth father was a member of the Igbo people from South Eastern Nigeria.

No wonder Blessing was concentrating. Lydia remem-bered the words her tutor used when they were learning the scope of the role the young officer faced.

'You're responsible for the scene,' she said, 'if you get a suspect to court, then every aspect will be scrutinised. One slip and a criminal might go free. Cock this up, and you have a black mark against you forever and a day. As soon as someone asks whether you're ready to step up to the next level, it will resurface. She can't handle the pressure.'

Lydia didn't envy Blessing's position one bit. Her role with the Crime Review Team didn't need her to use many of the skills she acquired during her degree course. As with thousands of other graduates, Lydia could earn a living without falling back on the subjects she studied.

"Everything covered so far?" Andy Carlton asked the young woman. Lydia thought she looked no more than twenty-one. Blessing clutched the clipboard to her ample chest as if it was a protective shield. She seemed too frightened to reply.

Geoff Mercer handed Blessing the car keys.

"Log these in, please, Sergeant. They're the spare set for DI Ferris's car. SOCO can check inside and outside for clues on where she went next."

"Thank you, Sir," she said, trying to juggle the keys and the clipboard to allow her to write. Lydia knew it was inevitable the ballpoint pen ended on the floor. She closed the gap between them and rescued the situation.

"Oh, thank you," she said, "I'm so nervous."

"Don't worry," said Lydia, "nobody died."

Blessing's large brown eyes widened with surprise. Who was this woman? Tall, elegant, and beautiful. The red hair colouring looked natural, and the corkscrew curls suited her. How could she be so relaxed and joking at a time such as this? An Inspector was missing.

"What have you recorded so far?" asked Lydia, "Who was the first officer attending? DI Carlton?"

"Yes, ma'am," said Blessing.

"Call me Lydia. I studied forensic psychology, but I'm attached to a cold case review team in Wiltshire. DI Carlton took control of the crime scene to ensure it was protected for the forensic people to work in safety. Do you have that listed, together with the appropriate time?"

"Twelve fifty-five," the younger girl replied, "and you and your boss arrived at ten past one."

"It was closer to a quarter past," whispered Lydia, "I checked my watch as we got to the top of the stairs."

Geoff Mercer and Andy Carlton organised the necessary photograph and video evidence. A fingertip search of the floor surrounding the car would follow in due course.

"Every crime scene is different," said Lydia as she and Blessing watched the experts at work. "Indoors, the limits of a search for evidence get defined by the layout of the various rooms and how they connect. Once you're in the wide outdoors, someone needs to decide a sensible boundary. A multi-storey car park poses its particular set of problems. Where was the van belonging to the kidnapper?"

"Was he parked up lying in wait?" suggested Blessing. "Or did he stop behind the car, blocking the exit? That gives the shortest distance needed to move her."

"The forensic people will tell us in time," said Lydia, "just relax, record everything, and it will be fine. The crime scene tape covers the most likely areas. As you said, he would park as close as he could get. My guess is directly opposite."

Blessing Umeh took a quick step back. The white line delineating the edge of the parking bay opposite Suzie's GTI was now clearly visible.

"You nearly put your foot in it then, Blessing," Lydia giggled.

"I'm always doing dumb things," she replied, "what's it like working with a cold case team?"

"A brilliant experience," said Lydia, "we've solved three murders in seven weeks. Our boss, Gus Freeman, is a genius. I thought we were on the verge of making it four out of four last Friday. I still haven't worked out why we didn't. Gus is such a deep thinker. He told me I had to learn to understand acceptance. Some things you can change, other things you can't. You take a view on whether what you've done has reached a level where you can live with it. Often it won't matter if you don't like what you see because unchangeable can be just that. I think I'll carry that insight with me to the grave. It applies to many areas of our lives, not just a crime we're investigating."

"I hope to move into positions where I work with people with that knowledge and experience," said Blessing. "most of the male detectives I meet are like DI Carlton. They resent the rise in the percentage of powerful women in the police force."

"I'm lucky to be working in a unit that doesn't harbour that bigotry," said Lydia. "The Crime Review Team is my first post since leaving university. I was lucky to get taken on considering the cutbacks."

"Where are you from?" asked Blessing.

"My family come from Scotland," said Lydia, "my birth mother, Eleanor, lives in Edinburgh, and my Mum and Dad are from Dundee. I only found my birth mother recently."

"Your father was Nigerian?"

"I'm not surprised you can tell," laughed Lydia, "the ginger hair might look Scottish, but the skin colour and my features tell the true story. He was a sailor who met my mother in the autumn of 1992 while his ship docked in the port of Leith. I plan to look for him with one of my colleagues. Well, he's more than a colleague."

"I wish you luck," said Blessing. "I was born in Warwick, and although my mother is easy-going, my father is strict. The menfolk in my family can appear very rude to English people. It's just their way. If your father doesn't want you to find him, what will you do?"

"I haven't thought that far ahead," said Lydia, "it's the hunt that interests me—searching for clues, just like in a murder case. If he wants nothing to do with me, that's cool. I'll know who he is at least, and that's what's driving me."

Blessing continued to make notes on her clipboard while they chatted. Lydia smiled to herself. Once Blessing had something else to think about besides how vital the task was and the fallout from getting it wrong, she relaxed into it and looked a natural.

It appeared DS Mercer and DI Carlton were winding up matters. The two senior officers left Suzie Ferris's abandoned car and joined them.

"The SOCO's have a few more items to gather, Sergeant," said Andy Carlton. "but DS Mercer is keen to head home to Devizes. Good meeting you, Lydia. We wish you both a safe trip back."

Lydia and Blessing said their goodbyes, and Geoff Mercer made for the stairway.

"Was I right, Sir?" asked Lydia, "did Gardiner wear gloves?"

"There were hundreds of prints on the door handles and the boot. Ninety-nine per cent of those will belong to DI Ferris or her family. We found nothing inside the car belonging to Suzie. No suitcase, handbag or other belongings. Gardiner must have removed them. The bay opposite was the location for the black van we believe he drove. Evidence from there might prove useful. They recovered hair, clothing fabric and skin fragments which suggest a scuffle took place. However, they could just as easily have come from a punch-up at the weekend. The spot in question fits if Gardiner drove into the parking space, overpowered Suzie and wrestled her into the back of the van. To move her from her GTI to the van would take a few seconds. Gardiner had every chance of achieving that without being seen."

"Could we look for the van leaving the car park on the cameras, Sir? It's barrier-controlled and pay-on-exit. A shame, because if St Peter's required drivers to enter their registration when they parked, that would help solve our problem."

"Andy Carlton is checking the CCTV coverage. We might get lucky and capture a registration, but Gardiner isn't stupid. My guess is he hired the van for the day, collected Suzie Ferris and, after taking her to wherever he's holding her, returned the van. That van will already have been cleaned and valeted for another hire on Saturday. Finding what he drove might not help one bit."

"Is there nothing more we can do?" asked Lydia.

Geoff Mercer could tell she felt frustrated.

"Time will tell whether Andy Carlton and his people unearth a clue," he said, "working with Gus Freeman is spoiling you. Active investigations can be this way. You gather hundreds of pieces of evidence for many hours without knowing whether any of it will prove useful."

"Back to the Crime Review Team office then?"

"Yes," said Geoff as they reached his Ford Kuga, "and pray Andy's team comes up with something. Either that or Gus uncovers a link we missed. Time marches on."

As they reversed out into the approach road to the car park, Geoff heard Lydia let out a big sigh.

"Don't let it get to you, Lydia. Andy Carlton and I don't work cases much differently from Gus Freeman. I know it's a while since I was on the front line, but I noticed things every day during the years I was a detective. So we're back to Gus's jigsaw and the pieces that don't fit. Most of what registered at the time proved useless, but I still noted them somewhere in my brain, and when similar situations arose, that back catalogue served me well. The pieces that didn't quite fit at the time needed something I'd seen or heard years earlier. That started me looking for a similar piece in the case I was currently handling. More often than not, I found it."

"So, you're saying Andy will recognise something in the evidence from St Peter's car park that reminds him of an earlier case. With luck, his back catalogue contains details of the missing piece we need to find."

"That's the size of it, Lydia. Give the office a ring to say we're on our way. We'll make it back before four o'clock if traffic's not too heavy."

Geoff headed for the motorway, and Lydia's thoughts returned to Suzie Ferris as she fished her phone out of her handbag.

If Geoff Mercer was right, the poor girl's life depended on the toss of a coin.

Chapter Five

SOON AFTER GUS returned from London Road, he decided it was time for another review.

Gus stood next to Alex's desk.

"What do you have for me?" he asked.

"I saw something interesting in Ricky Gardiner's biography, guv," said Alex.

Gus moved to the wallboard.

"Show me," he said.

"Ricky's a Londoner, born and bred. I can't find evidence of him living any further than twenty miles from the City. His parents split up when Ricky was eighteen. His father lived in Lewisham for the rest of his life. George Gardiner died in 2001 aged sixty-four. Ricky's mother moved around the country. She never re-married but had a string of relationships. They were with blokes with lots of money. Angie Gardiner died in January, aged seventy-six. At the time of her death, she owned three properties. A hotel on the seafront in Bude, Cornwall. An apartment in St

Paul's Square, Birmingham, and a detached house in a place called Leek Wootton where she lived alone."

"Why does that name sound familiar?" asked Gus.

"The Leek Wootton headquarters has been the Warwickshire Police force's home since 1949. It was a country house used by US armed forces during World War II. They adapted it for business use later."

"I remember it now. Didn't Warwickshire Police plan to sell it after the merger with West Mercia?"

"Yes, guv, the forces merged services including firearms and police dog officers in 2013. The building is only ten minutes from Mrs Gardiner's house."

"Check whether Ricky inherited the house. His mother's will might have cut him out of everything. It doesn't appear Ricky spent much time with his mother in the past thirty-five years. On the other hand, if he did inherit the lot, Gardiner's a wealthy man and that detached house could be where he took Suzie. Did you just stumble on this?"

"Sorry, guv. I wrote it on the board first thing this morning, but I didn't realise its significance. I wanted to get every piece of Gardiner's background available before you started analysing it. The house is only a five-minute drive from Leamington Spa."

"For crying out loud, Alex," Gus exploded.

Gus slammed his fist onto the desk.

"Suzie's life could depend on that information. Geoff Mercer and Lydia have been in Leamington for less than half an hour. We sent them on what will be a wild goose chase. The only positive they're likely to bring back is a time when John Ferris can expect her Golf GTI to arrive at the farm on the back of a low-loader."

Alex slumped back in his chair. He knew he'd messed up. His concentration was negligible these days.

"Neil," said Gus, "I know you're busy, but drop everything and check this will of Angie Gardiner's out for me, please? Call me if you get confirmation that Gardiner has keys to the property."

"On it, guv," said Neil Davis.

"I can't sit on my hands waiting around," said Gus, "I need to be doing something. Luke, I want you with me in Leek Wootton. We'll assess the situation during the journey."

"Happy to oblige, guv, as always," said Luke Sherman, pushing his chair back and preparing to leave.

"I can't believe Gardiner could resist using a house on the Warwickshire Police's doorstep to hold Suzie," said Gus. "He would enjoy sticking two fingers up at his former employers."

"That house is the logical option, guv," agreed Neil.

Gus looked around the room. What was needed in place to keep things running while he was away?

"Amelia, I want you to help Neil while we're gone. If we pass DS Mercer en route, please update him on where I've gone when he arrives here."

"Yes, guv," said Amelia, happy to be working with Neil once more.

"Reassure Geoff that Luke and I won't barge in without back-up, Amelia," said Gus, "once I receive confirmation from Neil, I'll contact Leek Wootton. They can organise a senior officer and an Armed Response Vehicle to meet us some distance from the property. We can't take any chances."

Amelia Cranston made a note of everything Gus wanted DS Mercer to hear.

"What do you want me to do, guv?" asked Alex.

"Go home, Alex," said Gus, "get yourself well. Don't

return until your head and body are right."

Gus and Luke left the office in a hurry.

Neil was on the phone to the Hub. They had to discover who now owned the property on the wallboard.

Amelia Cranston stared after Alex Hardy as he limped his way to the lift and waited for it to return to the first floor. He looked like a broken man. Amelia wondered why he didn't defend himself from Gus Freeman's attack. She'd caught the last snatches of conversation before DS Mercer took her home yesterday.

Alex told Gus the board contained part of Gardiner's background if he wanted to take a look. Lydia jumped in with her comment about sending the files to the ACC relating to their last case. Gus congratulated Alex for getting that task completed and said he'd study the board later. Every team member was on edge. It was understandable that mistakes occurred.

The office was suddenly quiet. First thing this morning, it was buzzing with activity as seven people tackled two very different cases. Only Neil and Amelia remained.

"Just you and me then, kiddo," said Neil, "let me bring you up to speed on how far Luke and I have reached. Then we can apply the finishing touches."

"I'm not as frightened by the confidential nature of this investigation as DS Mercer thinks," said Amelia. "If the evidence we gather means prison for someone whose actions stain the entire police family's reputation, then so be it. It's the right thing to do."

LUKE SHERMAN PERSUADED Gus to let him drive them to Leek Wootton when they reached the ground floor.

"You're in no fit state to drive, guv," said Luke, "it

matters to you that DI Ferris gets released unharmed, doesn't it? Your reactions in the office throughout yesterday and this morning emphasised that."

"You're right, Luke. I'm livid Alex didn't spot how vital the address was for this property belonging to Gardiner's late mother. Even if it turned out Mrs Gardiner left everything to a dog's home, we could have eliminated it from our search before Geoff Mercer headed for Leamington. It was sloppy."

"Alex is a good copper," said Luke, "the injury he suffered was severe, and I can see he's pushing himself too hard too soon. He doesn't want to let you down by admitting he's struggling with the pain."

"Neil commented on the number of pills he's taking, didn't he?" said Gus. "I've never asked Alex what the doctors have prescribed for him. Perhaps I should have."

"I think you have enough worries, for now, guv," said Luke, "sit back and relax. Let me take the strain. I'll use the motorway route to the Midlands, the same as DS Mercer. We can leave the M5 at Worcester and then make our arrangements with our colleagues in Warwickshire. Estimated time of arrival at Leek Wootton is three-thirty."

Gus stared through the windscreen as Luke propelled them over mile after mile of motorway tarmac at seventy miles per hour. At this time of day, they were lucky to be moving so quickly. He went through the list of tasks that might lay ahead if they discovered Suzie at the Leek Wootton address.

Suzie could need medical attention. What if Ricky Gardiner harmed her on Friday when he kidnapped her?

How was Gardiner holding Suzie inside the house? The ARV crew would carry a big red key to break through any external or internal doors. They might need bolt-cutters, too; Gus soon found himself with a lengthy list.

Luke's comment about his attitude towards Suzie's capture surprised him at first. The more he thought, he remembered that Luke was on security duty outside the bungalow after the break-in. Gus's role in the investigation into Frank North's murder put his life in danger. The ACC had agreed to twenty-four-hour surveillance.

It made sense that both Rick Chalmers and Luke knew that Suzie Ferris slept there.

Nothing happened that night, but the note Gus found on the kitchen table the following day revealed how close it had been and how intent Suzie was on getting her man. Unfortunately, Luke and Rick were on other duties well before the Bank Holiday weekend. No way could either of them know what followed.

Luke was no fool, though, and Gus knew that his feelings for Suzie shone through everything he'd done since he received that phone call on Monday morning. Nobody could accuse him of being professional. Gus shook his head. What was he thinking?

"OK, guv?" asked Luke, "we're making excellent progress. Another thirty minutes before you should make that call. Let's hope Neil calls back soon."

"He'd better," said Gus. "What you said earlier, Luke, about DI Ferris. I have the utmost respect for her."

"None of my business, guv," said Luke. "It was Emily Dickinson, wasn't it? *The heart wants what it wants, or else it doesn't care.*"

"No idea," said Gus, "it's a mess, whatever it is. I have dated Vera, the ACC's PA, for several weeks, and a woman half my age bursts into my life out of the blue. I've never had women fighting over me, Luke, and at sixty-two, I never thought it possible."

Luke laughed. Gus wasn't sure this was appropriate given the danger Suzie was in, let alone the relationship difficulties he was experiencing.

"I'm sorry, guv," said Luke, wiping tears from his eyes. "I've never had women fighting over me either. My partner, Nicky, wouldn't stand for it."

You learn something new every day, thought Gus. When the team mulled over arrangements for a team night out when this craziness was over, Neil suggested Luke accompanied Amelia Cranston, as they were both single. Luke replied by asking Neil why he thought he didn't have a partner to bring? It appeared that he did. If only his life were that simple.

SEVERAL CONVERSATIONS WERE in progress at London Road HQ in different parts of the building.

Vera Butler and Kassie Trotter were delivering cups of tea to offices on the admin floor. As they moved from room to room, they fretted over Suzie Ferris's whereabouts. What could have happened? Where did Geoff Mercer disappear to today, and what was Gus Freeman doing?

The ACC mentioned a family emergency to explain Geoff's absence, but Vera knew Christine was okay. She'd seen her shopping in The Brittox at lunchtime. It was bizarre.

Kassie was more concerned over her chocolate sponge. She would have two large slices left now with Mr Mercer away.

Further along the corridor, the ACC had been caught

without Geoff Mercer to protect him. Peter Morgan took advantage of Geoff's absence to drop in for a chat.

The ACC knew how insufferable Morgan could be. The Police Surgeon had no dead bodies to examine. If only a juicy murder landed on his desk, thought Kenneth Truelove, then he could get rid of him. The ACC remembered poor DI Ferris and prayed that Mercer and Freeman discovered her whereabouts and found her safe and sound.

"We appear to be lighter in number than usual," said Peter, interrupting the ACC's reverie.

"Sorry," said the ACC, "what do you mean?"

"Geoff Mercer and Suzie Ferris are both missing."

"What makes you think they're missing?" asked the ACC.

"Not missing. I mean, not here at work as one might expect on a Tuesday afternoon. I assume they're working together on a special case. Am I right?"

The ACC knew his next words were most likely to find their way into the Chief Constable's ear, but Morgan was getting on his nerves.

"Peter, whatever they're involved in has bugger all to do with you. Why don't you get back to your office and mind your own business?"

As the door slammed behind the fleeing Peter Morgan, the ACC smiled. Now he knew what 'high dudgeon' meant.

"Why didn't I do that half an hour ago," he said to himself as he resumed his regular spot by the window.

On the other side of the building, the Chief Constable was troubled. Sandra Plunkett was on a conference call with a difference. It wasn't an official phone line.

"I'm not convinced we made the correct decision last Friday," she said.

"It was the best option at the time," said Dominic Culverhouse, "and we both agreed."

"I did what you wanted," said Ricky Gardiner. "The woman's safe and sound. What's Freeman doing? Has he spoken to the others about your little problem?"

"He can't have. My source convinced me we would know if he had," said Sandra Plunkett. "I think your message frightened Freeman. He wasn't his usual self when he came here today. The Crime Review Team has started work on their next cold case. That suggests Freeman took heed of your warning."

"Look, Sandra," said Culverhouse, "Terry Davis can't pose a threat now, and our secret died with him. We have nothing to fear. You, Ricky, on the other hand, allowed yourself to get caught on camera. Freeman could have only told Mercer and that worm, Truelove, that he'd found proof since their last meeting that Davis's death wasn't an accident. Freeman must know you murdered Davis. You are the one in danger, not us. How you handle that fact is up to you. You still have the girl. She might be your only way out of this mess. I believe this finishes our business with you. Sandra and I will deny all knowledge of any transaction ever taking place. The money is untraceable. I made sure of that."

"You'll regret casting me adrift, Culverhouse," said Ricky Gardiner, "if I go down, you're going with me."

With that, Ricky Gardiner left the conference call.

"Are we in trouble?" asked Sandra.

"Destroy anything that links you to Gardiner," said Culverhouse, "I've already done so at my end, but it won't hurt to double-check. The money we paid Gardiner isn't a problem, as I told him. The real threat was that Freeman learned the truth of what happened six years ago. We covered our tracks well, and nothing that Davis uncovered will ever come to light."

"Why did I agree to Gardiner kidnapping Suzie Ferris?" moaned Sandra, "that was unnecessary. If Freeman had nothing on us, why use her as a bargaining tool?"

"Gardiner was in the village where Freeman lives before he killed Terry Davis. He saw Suzie arrive at the bungalow after her session in the Lamb with this old boyfriend, Yarwood, or whatever his name was. Ricky knew Suzie never left the bungalow until noon on Saturday at the earliest. That made Freeman vulnerable. We agreed to use that against him. If by a miracle, he had learned about Oakley, then Ricky's threat would be genuine. I would let Ricky kill Ferris to protect the two of us, Sandra. We stick to the same story as we devised six years ago. Don't lose your resolve now. We're both in line for a promotion that takes us one step nearer our goal. I won't let anything or anyone get in the way. You'd do well to remember that."

Sandra Plunkett was holding a dead phone.

Culverhouse had gone. Sandra sat and considered what he said. Had he just threatened to kill her? Sandra realised she was shaking. What wouldn't she give to have Naomi here to hold her and tell her everything would be alright?

"WE CAN USE the M42 and Warwick bypass nearly to the front door of the police station, guv," said Luke, "we've made good time."

"I want to avoid going there if possible, Luke. I need us to stop just once. Find somewhere near the Gardiner property where we can wait for Neil's call. The cavalry won't have far to come once we get the green light."

"I'll find a place on the same approach road they'll use.

Hill Wootton Road looks favourite. Neil was checking those details you wanted through the Hub. It shouldn't take long."

Minutes later, Luke spotted a lay-by and drew up beside a large white removals van which shielded them from view from the road. They sat and waited until an incoming call broke the silence. Gus grabbed his phone.

"Yes, Neil?" he barked.

"Exactly as you thought, guv," said Neil, "the Hub confirmed that when Angie Gardiner died in January, everything passed to her only son, Richard George Gardiner. Both the hotel in Bude and the luxury apartment in Birmingham are up for sale. The Leek Wootton address was Angie's home until she died. Her solicitors received no instructions from Gardiner regarding that property. The address they have on file for Gardiner is a post office in Lewisham. I could dig deeper to see if he has a fixed abode. I'm sure he's got a place in London somewhere."

"Leave that for now, Neil. You and Amelia should concentrate on closing the net on Culverhouse and Plunkett."

"Got it, guv. One last thing, the call from Gardiner on Monday morning was from a burner phone, as you expected. No way of identifying where it originated. Sorry."

Gus ended the call and dialled the Leek Wootton HQ number.

MEANWHILE, Geoff Mercer parked his Ford Kuga in Gus Freeman's spot below the CRT office. He and Lydia went upstairs in the lift. Their trip to Leamington and back was at an end. How much good it achieved was still in the balance.

Geoff found Neil Davis and Amelia Cranston hard at work.

"Where are the others?" he asked.

"Gus and Luke drove to Leek Wootton, Sir," said Neil, "and DS Hardy got sent home."

Geoff and Lydia sat. What the heck had they missed?

Neil took them through how things unfolded after they left. Amelia passed on the additional details Gus Freeman left for Geoff Mercer from the notes she'd made.

Geoff and Lydia listened in stunned silence. Lydia wanted to call Alex straight away.

"So, you've just called Gus telling him that this Leek Wootton detached house is where Gardiner is probably holding Suzie Ferris?"

"I got off the phone less than five minutes ago," said Neil. "Did you find useful clues in the car park, Sir?"

"We found Suzie's car, Neil. I suppose that's something. Forensics were thorough in their evidence gathering. DI Carlton and his team have a set of DI Ferris's keys. I'm not sure how soon it will get returned."

"I'm worried about Alex," said Lydia. She was on the verge of tears.

Geoff Mercer made a mental note to ask Gus whether something was happening between those two.

"Alex should have stayed in his wheelchair for another month at least," said Neil, "he's struggled this past couple of weeks with those crutches."

"He mentioned that he'd found something interesting concerning the house," said Amelia, "but he didn't respond when Gus lost his temper."

"What do you mean?" asked Geoff.

Amelia told him what she had heard.

"I wasn't concentrating," said Geoff, "I missed that

entirely. No matter. I wasn't here to correct Gus. Let's park that for now. If Gus follows the plan he outlined, then with confirmation of ownership of the property, he should be in touch with Warwickshire Police. We can only wait to hear what they find when they break down the door. Let's hope Suzie can get released unharmed."

"Amelia and I are ready to tie up the final items on the Oakley case, Sir," said Neil.

"Excellent. I should hold off going through your findings until Gus is here. Make sure everything's ready before you leave tonight. Tomorrow, I want you and Lydia to start on the new cold case. Everything must appear to be proceeding as normal."

"Understood," said Neil.

"Will you need me tomorrow, Sir?" asked Amelia.

"That depends on Gus Freeman," said Geoff, "and how things turn out in Leek Wootton."

SUZIE FERRIS WAS THIRSTY. It had been ages since breakfast. What wouldn't she give for a cold beer right now? She guessed it was mid-afternoon. She'd heard the man moving around in the kitchen for a while after he'd collected the breakfast tray. He'd left the house earlier this afternoon and driven away. When he returned, she heard his footsteps upstairs, but he had brought nothing for her to eat or drink. It was quiet in the house. Not that she was complaining. At least he was leaving her alone. None of it made any sense. Why was she even here?

WHEN GUS RANG the Warwickshire Police, he got put through to Detective Chief Inspector Oliver Pinnock. Gus ran through his usual spiel, explaining who he was, when the DCO interrupted him.

"This relates to the St Peter's car park affair in Leamington that DI Andy Carlton updated me on, I take it?"

"My boss, DS Geoff Mercer, was on that part of the case, Sir. He thought a consultant was the wrong person to send."

"Quite, so what's the current status?"

"We have confirmation that Ricky Gardiner, who's wanted for murder in Devizes, is the owner of a detached house four miles up the road from you, Sir. To keep us off his back, he kidnapped one of Geoff Mercer's detectives last Friday afternoon. She'd recently completed a cyber-crime course in Ryton-on-Dunsmore."

"Ye gods and little fishes. He sounds like a nasty piece of work. Why is his name familiar?"

"Gardiner was one of us, Sir. He worked for the Met and spent more than half his career undercover. He's a gun for hire now in the private sector."

"You can fill me in on who he killed and why later. It sounds vital that we get to the property, capture this villain and release DS Mercer's detective before Gardiner can cause any more harm. Is the girl in danger, do you think?"

"He threatened to kill Suzie Ferris when he contacted us on Monday morning."

"That's all I need, Freeman. I'll get an Armed Response Vehicle to you in ten minutes maximum. Your contact will be Mike Farrell. He will bring a team of three with him. DI Carlton advised me that Gardiner operated alone. Do you concur?"

"He's a lone wolf, Sir. He might not come quietly, but he'll be the only one to handle."

"I think you can rely on Mike Farrell to make sure he

comes quietly, and I shouldn't need to remind you that Gardiner's the only one *they'll* have to handle. So it would be best if you stood aside until Mike gives the all-clear to enter the property. Is that understood?"

"Of course, Sir. Force of habit," said Gus.

"Forty years of service does that to a chap, Freeman," said DCI Pinnock, "I'm out next year. I won't be in a rush to return to the fray, unlike you. Give me the address, and good hunting."

"186 Woodman Lane, Sir. We're in a lay-by on the approach road. We'll tag along behind as soon as we see your ARV."

Oliver Pinnock thanked Gus and ended the call.

"That's a relief," said Luke, "I wondered whether they needed to carry out a risk assessment first."

"Cheeky," said Gus, "that's my line. Keep watch for them. They should appear on our left in a few minutes."

"Here they come," said Luke six minutes later. "They're not hanging around, but at least they aren't announcing our arrival with sirens and flashing lights."

Luke started the car and moved away from his spot beside the removals van. He followed the ARV along Woodman Lane. The vehicle stopped twenty yards short of the entrance to the property. The doors opened, and four men exited the vehicle dressed from head to foot in dark clothing.

They wore helmets with face shields and soft-armour body protectors, and three carried Heckler and Koch rifles. The front man held what looked like a Sig Sauer handgun. Luke was unsure, at this distance, whether it was the old P229 or the P320. Both weapons were more than useful when push came to shove. Luke wished he had his Glock 17 in a shoulder strap, but despite the terror threat and rampant organised crime, the authorities still resisted the call for officers to carry arms at all times.

Gus was out of the car and following before Luke could release his seat belt.

"Hell's bells, guv," he said, "do you have a death wish?"

Luke decided it was pointless trying to stop Gus, so he followed him.

The team leader glanced behind his crew and saw Gus and Luke creeping along the lane. They could see an empty driveway through the trees at the front of the property.

"Gus Freeman, I presume?" said the team leader.

Gus nodded.

"Mike Farrell. My gaffer said you might be trouble. Jammy, stay here and keep these two jokers out of harm's way. Andy Carlton mentioned a black van. Any ideas?"

"Gardiner probably hired it for the occasion," said Gus, looking at Mike Farrell over a rifle barrel. He wasn't going anywhere while Jammy stood in front of him.

"We'll assume he's inside then," said Mike, "Chris, can you fetch the ram, please? That oak door looks solid. You might have to swing it more than once."

"Can we gain access to the rear?" asked Luke.

"And you are?" asked Mike Farrell.

"DS Luke Sherman. Firearms trained, I met Mr Freeman on his security detail last month. I'm now on temporary assignment with his Crime Review Team."

"Security detail? Trouble follows you around, Gus, doesn't it?" asked Farrell.

"I don't encourage it," Gus said.

"Deepak, you and Sherman make your way along the right-hand side of the house as Chris approaches the front door. The shutters restrict vision for people both inside and outside the house. We still have the element of surprise. If the oak door slows us, you can force an entry; any way you wish. Kick in the back door or smash through the French windows. Just get inside fast."

Chris darted from the cover of the trees, and Mike was right behind him in the driveway. Two lusty blows with the big red key, and the door opened. Mike Farrell raced inside with gun raised, shouting, "Armed police. Armed police."

Deepak gave the back door a nudge with the butt of his rifle, and he and Luke were inside the kitchen in seconds.

"Clear!" cried Deepak. The same cry echoed around the house as Chris and Jammy checked the upstairs rooms and shouted to Mike Farrell. Their calls covered a muffled cry from somewhere in the house.

Mike Farrell and Gus stood in the hallway and listened. The only room left was the padlocked front room.

"Help, I'm in here."

"Suzie? Are you OK?" shouted Gus.

"Oh, Gus. Thank God."

"Stand clear of the door, Miss," shouted Mike Farrell.

Chris and Jammy were now in the hallway. Chris picked up the discarded ram by the broken front door, and the padlock spun along the passage leading to the kitchen. Deepak and Luke stood to one side as it flew past them.

Mike Farrell led the way inside the room. Suzie stood in the middle of the room, her handcuffed wrists in front of her.

She looked a mess and smelled worse, but Gus thought she was the most beautiful sight he'd ever seen.

"Let's see what we can do with these cuffs," said Mike. "Why am I not surprised? This style was the standard issue a decade ago. I've got a set of keys to fit that lock. We'll have you out in no time."

Gus was looking around the room.

"Sorry," said Suzie, "the cleaner doesn't come until Wednesday."

"Where's Gardiner?" asked Gus.

"Who?" asked Suzie, "I've no idea who brought me here or why. He drove off around lunchtime. He returned a couple of hours later and left again after spending time upstairs."

Mike Farrell glanced towards Chris and Jammy.

They shook their heads.

"The only items I saw upstairs belong to the young lady, Sir," said Jammy, "they were lying on the bed in the spare room."

"Gardiner's on his toes," said Mike, "something spooked him."

"Or someone warned him we were on our way," said Gus.

"I wish I knew what was going on," said Suzie. "More than anything, I wish this house wasn't a crime scene. I'd love to run upstairs to take a shower and change my clothes, and I itch everywhere."

"We'll take you back to the station and get a doctor to check you first," said Mike Farrell. "We need to photograph your minor injuries and collect forensic evidence. I don't know why I'm explaining this to you. You know the procedure. You'll be with us for several hours yet, DI Ferris, while we complete the necessary tasks. We need a statement from you, but after everything you've been through, that can wait until later."

"You're all heart," said Suzie.

The only thing Suzie wanted was to have Gus hold her and then call her parents. She sighed, knowing the police had a job to do. There was no point complaining.

"Did he harm you, Suzie?" asked Gus.

"Come on now, Freeman," said Farrell, "we must follow protocol."

"Can you ring my parents, Gus? Tell them I'm fine and can't wait to get home to see them."

"Of course," said Gus. "We found your car earlier today, by the way. Once forensics have finished, they'll arrange to get it home."

"I suppose things will get back to normal in time," said Suzie. "After I've turned cartwheels for this gentleman here, I hope to catch up with you. Perhaps, you can tell me why this Gardiner kidnapped me, and who might have a reason to warn him that help was on its way?"

"I wouldn't mind learning that too, Miss," said Mike Farrell, "we're as much in the dark as you."

"I can't speak for Luke," said Gus, "but I'm not going anywhere. If we need to stay until midnight before we can get you home, so be it."

Mike Farrell could see it was pointless arguing. So he called Leek Wootton and requested that DCI Oliver Pinnock send a forensic team to Woodman Lane. As soon as they arrived, Mike Farrell led Suzie outside.

Jammy brought the ARV to the front door. Minutes later, Suzie was on her way to Leek Wootton. Chris and Deepak remained to control the site in the unlikely event Gardiner returned.

Luke Sherman followed the ARV at a polite distance, with Gus sitting beside him. Luke knew Gus would want to be involved in whatever happened next.

It remained to be seen whether the DCI and Mike Farrell could stop him.

Chapter Six

WHEN GUS and Luke arrived at Leek Wootton, they learned that DI Ferris was with the medical staff.

"How long?" asked Gus.

"It can often take an hour, Sir," he was told by an officious desk sergeant.

Gus sat on the nearest chair. Luke sat next to him.

"I assume we're making a point, guv?"

"We're not leaving here until I hear what Suzie says, so yes, I'm making a point."

"I heard you speaking to her father on the phone as we made our way here. I imagine her parents are over the moon?"

"Only to be expected, Luke. Suzie isn't their only child but their only daughter and precious. John Ferris kept thanking me, but I played a minor role in locating and rescuing her."

Luke watched the clock on the wall. It was still only six o'clock. So much had happened since they reached that lay-by near Woodman Lane at half-past three.

"Do you think anyone will still be working in the CRT office, guv?" he asked.

"Not if they've got any sense," said Gus. "I know what you're thinking. I suppose I should call Geoff Mercer and update him."

Gus made the call. Geoff picked up straight away.

"Gus? What's the latest? Did you catch Gardiner at the house? Is Suzie safe?"

"Suzie's fine. The doctor's checking her over now to be certain. As for Gardiner, something, or someone, spooked him. He left the house thirty minutes before we arrived."

"Damn him," said Geoff, "are the Warwickshire people searching for his black van?"

"We don't know if the black van is relevant, Geoff. Gardiner could have been driving another vehicle. Luke and I will keep pressing for action at this end. If we learn more in the next few hours, I'll get the details to you. I'd prefer us to be the ones to apprehend him, but it might not be the wisest choice. I doubt he's anywhere in the Midlands area now, anyway. A rat returns to its lair. Gardiner will have run to London. How did you get on in Leamington? While I'm on the phone, what's happening back there in the CRT office?"

"One thing at a time, Gus. We must have passed you on the motorway. Lydia and I arrived in the office around four. Apart from the GTI, we found nothing likely to be crucial, especially since you've rescued Suzie. It will merely add to the evidence against Gardiner when we catch him. Neil brought us up to speed on matters between you and DS Hardy. Amelia is working with Neil on the Oakley business. If you can drag yourself away from Leek Wootton, then first thing tomorrow Neil will present us with the evidence he, Luke and Amelia have compiled over the past couple of days."

"I'll make it back for that. I look forward to hearing about it. Any reaction from London Road?" asked Gus.

"Nothing to trouble us. Lydia has set up your so-called Freeman Files for the next cold case. Neil and Lydia will start work on that tomorrow after the presentation. Again, I've stressed the need to imply that everything is normal."

"Is Lydia still there?"

"I sent her home at five. She was eager to check on Alex Hardy."

"Before you ask, I've had a word with both of them," said Gus, "they know the rules. Lydia isn't a serving officer, so she deserves a little latitude. As for Alex, well…"

"Amelia tells me you missed Alex telling you about the house earlier in the day. Several people were speaking at once. You chose the priority item at the time, and the invitation to look at the incomplete wallboard slipped your mind. It's nobody's fault. We were under pressure."

"I may need to mend fences then," said Gus, "but I stand by my decision to send Alex home. I don't want him back until he's well enough to give us his total attention."

"Fair enough, you know him better than I do," said Geoff. "I was ready to head home when you called. What's next for Suzie?"

"A shower and a change of clothes," said Gus, "Gardiner denied her both. It appears he fed her and kept her handcuffed throughout the ordeal. She had no clue who Gardiner was or why he took her. I'm hoping they'll let me listen to her interview."

"Would it help if I rang and put in a good word?" asked Geoff.

"I'm dealing with a DCI called Oliver Pinnock," said

Gus, "he seems a decent chap. Pinnock might take notice of the ACC, but *you'll* get short shrift."

"Hilarious," said Geoff.

"That wasn't a dig about your height, Geoff," said Gus.

"I bet. We'll see you in the morning, yes?"

"I'm hoping we can reunite her with her family as soon as they've interviewed Suzie. Then, Luke can drive the three of us back. He's had a quiet day."

Gus heard Geoff Mercer chuckling as he ended the call.

"Excuse me, Sir," said the desk sergeant. "The DCI asked me to tell you that the satellite room in the interview suite is available for you if you wish. They're starting in five minutes."

"Thank you," said Gus, "come on, Luke, let's hear what Suzie has to say."

Five minutes later, after Pinnock completed the usual preliminaries, Suzie retraced her steps from when she left the Ibis Hotel on Friday morning. Gus noticed the bandages on her wrists covering the damage done by the constant chafing of the handcuffs. The cuts and abrasions on her arms and legs would heal in time. The psychological trauma could take much longer to overcome.

Gus half-listened as she told Pinnock about getting petrol at the garage and noticing a man by the coffee machine. He was glad to see how much better Suzie looked now that she was clean and wearing fresh clothes. Gus watched as she pushed her hair behind her ears. Clearly, she was concentrating hard, not wanting to miss out on an important fact.

Luke sensed Gus wince when Suzie described the moment Gardiner attacked her in the car park. Gus sat up to take more notice as Suzie described their journey before arriving at the house in Woodman Lane.

Suzie told Pinnock that she forced herself to remember a sequence of roundabouts, traffic lights, schools and a church clock chiming the hour as they drove past. Suzie realised it was a desperate attempt to stop herself from imagining what might happen to her rather than being helpful to people hunting for her.

"Based on the time they were on the move, Gardiner drove around sixty extra miles to confuse Suzie," said Gus. "He realised she'd try to calculate where he'd taken her. In the end, his mother's old place was only ten minutes from the car park."

Gus and Luke listened to Suzie's account of her four days in that darkened front room.

DCI Pinnock asked her about her captor. What did he do during the day? Did Gardiner come into the room? Had he touched her? Did he say anything to show who was behind the kidnapping, or was he working alone?

"Gardiner never spoke," said Suzie. "When we reached the house on Friday afternoon, I tried to escape. The van stopped. He opened the back door and released the hand-cuff from the van wall. He secured my arms in front of me, and as he led me out of the van, I jumped forward, pulled the bag from my head and started yelling. I ran as fast as I could. I kept telling myself he was twenty years older than me. There was no way he should catch me, but he clipped my ankles just as I thought I'd made it, and when I face-planted the tarmac, I hurt like hell. What did he do all day? He opened the door just far enough to slide in a tray with tea and toast in the mornings. If I needed the loo, he escorted me across the hallway and back. Later in the day, he opened the door to place a takeaway meal just inside on the floor. There was always a drink on the tray, plus a meal. That was it. I heard him moving around from time to time.

He listened to the radio. Apart from leaving during the late afternoon or evening to fetch food, he never went out. Nobody visited the house. I never heard him speaking with anyone on the phone, but he could have gone upstairs or into the garden to prevent me from overhearing any conversation. There was never any contact between us other than that. I thought he would rape me and maybe kill me in the first twenty-four hours. Why did he take me otherwise? Gardiner didn't know me. I didn't know him. With whom *could* he have been working? The only day his routine altered was today, when he went out earlier than usual, returned without the takeaway and then went out again. I didn't realise he'd gone for good."

"What can you tell us about the van?" asked Pinnock.

"It was black, with a metal frame on the inside. That's where Gardiner already had the handcuffs in place. He slammed me on the van floor, put the bag over my head, so I never saw his face, flipped me onto my back and cuffed me."

"When you escaped from him at the house, did you see the van then?"

"I managed to get the bag off my face as I ran away. Then I looked everywhere for a way to escape, searching for someone to help me. When he marched me back to the house - wait, he bent and picked up the cloth bag as we walked back to the driveway. I saw my case, handbag and shopping on the front seat. It was a Mercedes Sprinter, but he got me indoors within seconds. I never caught the registration. It looked new."

"No markings on the side of the van?"

"A van hire name with an 01926 number. Sorry, I can't be any more specific."

"What about the sound of the van engine? It must have

left an impression if you had travelled for a couple of hours. On the occasions that Gardiner left the house, did the engine always sound the same?"

Gus watched as Suzie closed her eyes. He shuffled his feet and moved position in his chair. Luke wondered what he was thinking.

Gus remembered lying awake and watching Suzie as she slept that Saturday morning after they returned from the shower. He'd wondered what he'd done to deserve someone wanting to give him so much pleasure.

"It was a different tone," said Suzie, "I was inside the van when it was moving, and that muted the sound. When he left on Saturday, the first thing I did was try to escape. I was listening for the engine noise in case he returned. Going over it again when he returned, it was quieter than before."

"He returned the Sprinter and either retrieved his vehicle from the van hire firm's compound or a car park close by," said Gus.

"Unless Suzie saw that vehicle, then we're in the dark as far as what he drove when he scarpered," said Luke.

"Did you ever catch sight of the vehicle through the shutters?" Oliver Pinnock asked.

"Gardiner parked the van in front of the house near the trees," said Suzie. "Anyone passing had to walk into the driveway to see it. I broke so many nails trying to escape on Saturday and Sunday that I gave up attacking the window locks. As for seeing a van or car in front of the window, I don't remember. I'm not much help, am I?"

"Everything you can remember will help us build a picture of Gardiner," said DCI Pinnock. "We have other avenues of enquiry to follow. Forensics will collect every scrap of evidence available from the property. He left in a hurry, so he didn't have time to remove every trace of his being there. We can put a recent photograph of him in front of every van hire firm owner in the Warwick area. Someone will recognise him, and if we're lucky, they'll know what vehicle he's driving. Unless he shredded every scrap of paper in the house, we could discover correspondence between him and the people behind your kidnapping. Gus Freeman insists Gardiner offers his services in the private sector these days. His attack wasn't personal. He was working for someone. We need to discover who that was. Unfortunately, he remembered to take his digital devices with him. Progress might be slow, but it will be in the right direction. If you think of something to add, call me in the coming days. I'll update your superiors on our progress. The best thing for you now is rest and recovery; I'm sure you want to get home to your family. Two people are waiting to help with that. Thank you for your co-operation, DI Ferris. May I say how glad we are here at Leek Wootton to see you safe and sound after your ordeal? We'll do every-thing we can to arrest Gardiner and bring him to justice."

"We want the same thing, Sir," said Suzie, "but tonight, all I want is to get home and sleep in my bed."

Gus and Luke left the satellite room and waited for Suzie to emerge. Oliver Pinnock walked her out, carrying her suitcase and her bags. He handed them to Luke Sherman.

"Safe journey home," he said, watching proceedings over Luke's shoulder.

"Thank you, Sir," said Luke. He turned to see what was so fascinating.

Gus Freeman stood with Suzie Ferris, clinging to him for dear life.

"Delayed shock," said Gus, as if that explained everything.

DCI Pinnock smiled and returned to his office.

"See you in a minute. I'll take these things to the car," said Luke.

"I thought I'd never see you again," said Suzie when they were alone.

"I'll never forget the message Gardiner delivered on Monday morning," said Gus as he wrapped her in his arms, "it sent a chill down my spine. You're safe, Suzie. That's all that matters."

"Do you think we can persuade Luke to look the other way?" she said as they walked outside arm in arm.

"In general, do you mean, or just while we're travelling home?" asked Gus.

"I've destroyed any chance of keeping us a secret now, haven't I? I couldn't wait for you to hold me in your arms again, even if a DCI was watching us back there. Don't leave me alone, Gus; I need you to sit in the back with me."

"I wasn't thinking of going anywhere else," said Gus.

Luke wasn't surprised when Gus and Suzie slipped into the back seat of his car.

"Home, Luke," said Suzie, "next stop, Worton. You know how to get to our farm, don't you?"

"I've driven past the entrance many times," he replied. "Look, if anyone asks me about what happened tonight, I'll tell them it was a natural reaction caused by a traumatic incident. Everyone needs a hug at a time such as that. If others read something extra into it, then I won't add fuel to the fire."

"Thanks, Luke," said Suzie, "we owe you a big drink."

Gus nudged Suzie to show her the text he'd sent her father. She knew a tearful reunion awaited. Suzie laid her head on Gus's shoulder and was asleep before they reached the M5 junction near Worcester.

Just two hours later, Luke turned into the long driveway leading to the Ferris farm.

"Wake up, sleepyhead," whispered Gus. Suzie stretched and ran a hand through her hair. As Luke parked the car, Suzie turned Gus's face towards her and kissed him.

"I'll thank you properly for getting me home later," she said. "My father won't let you stay tonight."

Jackie Ferris was hovering by the car door. She couldn't wait to hug her daughter. John Ferris stood watching and waiting as mother and daughter cried on one another's shoulders.

He nodded to Gus. "Thank you, Gus," he said, "I don't know what we would have done if things had turned out differently."

"The biggest vote of thanks goes to the Warwickshire Police," said Gus, "Luke and I were just along for the ride."

"Come on inside," said Jackie, "you must be tired. Have you eaten?"

"I'm starving," said Suzie, "but please don't say it'll have to be a takeaway. I've had my fill of those for a while."

Luke looked at Gus. When did they last eat? For him, it was breakfast, which was close to sixteen hours ago. But, despite it being almost ten o'clock at night, he wouldn't refuse a bite to eat.

John Ferris waved an arm, encouraging them to move inside the kitchen. Jackie must have started work soon after hearing they were leaving Leek Wootton. The barley risotto with butternut squash was light and nourishing. Gus, Luke and Suzie didn't need Jackie to ask twice when she offered a second helping.

"I'm itching to open a bottle of champagne," said John Ferris, "but coffee will be far more sensible. We can celebrate another time."

"I ought to head home, guv," said Luke.

"You get off," said John Ferris, "I can run Gus home in the Land Rover."

Luke said his goodbyes and left them alone.

"Right then, Gus," said John, "what can you tell us?"

"The investigation I mentioned yesterday is still ongoing, I'm afraid. I can't breathe a word. When I get to work tomorrow, I hope to learn our enquiries are complete. Everything will soon be out in the open after that."

"I wish I understood what it was about," said Suzie.

"I need to speak with you, Suzie," said Gus. "It's only right you understand why Gardiner targeted you."

Jackie Ferris finished loading the dishwasher and tidying her kitchen.

"I'll get off to bed," she said, "and leave you two to talk. John, fetch the Land Rover."

"It's only across the yard."

"It's never stopped you from taking five minutes over it before. Find something to look at outside for a while."

Suzie and Gus soon found themselves alone.

"I think they like you," said Suzie.

"I got that impression when I arrived here on horseback the other morning. John and Jackie are good people, Suzie. The same age as me if you hadn't noticed."

"Very funny. Spill the beans, Gus."

"Okay," said Gus, "but listen, don't interrupt me with questions. Some I don't have the answers to, and your Dad will be revving the engine on the Land Rover in two minutes."

"Agreed."

"The Chief Constable sent you to the College of Policing on Tuesday the eighth. She told you not to take your smartphone or your laptop. That was significant. It didn't stop you from calling your mother on the hotel land-line on Friday to say you weren't driving home. However, it did mean you were out of the loop for events in Devizes over that first weekend. Terry Davis flew home from Marbella to visit Neil on Friday evening. The trip was to celebrate Melody's pregnancy. Terry was looking forward to becoming a grandfather."

"What do you mean? He was."

"No interruptions, you agreed."

"Sorry."

"Over the previous ten days, Ricky Gardiner was watching my bungalow. Because the CRT was so successful, his handlers worried we might stumble on something they wanted to stay buried. It's my fault for turning over random stones to see what crawls out. One case often isn't enough to keep me occupied. They paid Gardiner to silence Terry when they learned he was in town. They couldn't risk him telling me anything. Late on Sunday night, Terry died from a fall down a fire escape at the rear of his hotel. The Chief Constable wanted Peter Morgan to rush the cause of death as an accident. Neil and I realised it was murder as soon as we saw the body. Last week, with Luke Sherman and a young WPC assisting us, we proved that Gardiner was our killer. You continued your course at the College without a clue that something had happened. Nobody could contact you. I tried calling without success."

Suzie took Gus's hands in hers.

"Yes, I was worried about you," he said. "I hadn't heard from you since Saturday lunchtime when you left my place. I didn't realise you never received my message."

"You thought I was ignoring you. Silly man. I missed you every day."

"We both know what's happened since Friday," said

Gus, "now you can understand why it was you that Gardiner kidnapped. He was snooping around in Urchfont over the Bank Holiday weekend and saw that you spent the night at my place. His handlers wanted to put the squeeze on me. If there was a chance Terry told me the secret he'd unearthed before he died, then if Gardiner was holding you, I couldn't pass that knowledge to Geoff Mercer and the ACC. Gardiner threatened to kill you when he called me on Monday morning. He and his employers knew you were too important to me."

"Are you saying that the Chief Constable's involved in this? She told me not to take my phone, so I would be unaware of what happened to Terry Davis. Why didn't I see it in the press or on TV?"

"The ACC agreed to run with the accidental death angle in his press conference. We didn't want Gardiner and the others alerted that Geoff Mercer was leading a murder enquiry. We had learned it was Monty Jennings who supplied Terry Davis with his up-to-date gossip from London Road. Jennings listened to Peter Morgan weekly in the White Bear, and the Police Surgeon loves to brag about things he's heard."

"I can't believe that of Monty," said Suzie, "poor Vera. Of course, Peter's a snob, so that bit doesn't come as a surprise."

"Vera didn't have a clue that Monty helped leak the gossip. She was never involved. Terry discovered something related to one of Monty's old business ventures, which gave him leverage. That happened even before Vera and Monty got together. Monty passed on information for years to stop Terry from dropping him in it with the law."

"I can see why my lack of a phone was part of the plan. I couldn't report suspicious activity, such as Gardiner following me into the College car park. You couldn't trace my whereabouts either via GPS on Friday afternoon when he first took me."

"We weren't even aware you were missing, Suzie. Because you stayed in the Midlands the previous weekend, John wasn't that worried. He and Jackie thought you were having fun with people you met on the course. He called me when you hadn't turned up by late Sunday evening. Even then, I didn't know it was a kidnapping until Gardiner passed his message on Monday morning."

"What does the Chief Constable have to do with this?"

"Terry Davis *did* pass on his secret before he died, if not in person. He left a cryptic message with one of his confidential informants. She passed it to Neil Davis, and together we solved the riddle. Sandra Plunkett and Dominic Culverhouse were Gardiner's handlers. They paid him to silence Terry Davis. Gardiner held you captive to prevent me from informing the ACC that Terry believed Plunkett and Culverhouse committed a crime six years ago."

"Culverhouse is at Portishead, isn't he? His name has come up on previous occasions. He ensured Terry carried the can for the cock-ups on the Trudi Villiers murder, even though he was one of her many lovers."

"I don't know if we have all the pieces of the jigsaw yet," said Gus, "tomorrow morning will be crucial. I want to be open and honest with you, and I hope you'll forgive me. Terry discovered that after they attended a ten-year reunion dinner for Bramshill graduates, Culverhouse and Plunkett hit and killed a cyclist. The hit-and-run never got reported. On Monday, when I received the call, I told the ACC we were hours away from getting enough evidence to bring charges. We already had enough to charge Gardiner for murder."

"You took a gamble," nodded Suzie, "that I was only in danger if the Chief Constable worked out you knew the truth. As long as you made it appear you abandoned the search for evidence and carried on with the team's normal duties, she had nothing to tell Culverhouse or Gardiner. There was nothing to cause them to panic."

"I believed the threat was genuine," said Gus, "and I'm sure Gardiner would go to any lengths to save his skin. Culverhouse, too, based on what I know of him. But, on the other hand, I'm not sure whether Sandra Plunkett is that ruthless. So I gambled that your life was only in danger if I talked to Geoff and the ACC about the hit-and-run, and they requested a full-scale investigation from the soft-shoe brigade."

"So, you carried on looking for evidence *and* started a search for me? Are Luke Sherman and this WPC still attached to your team? Who is she, by the way?"

"Amelia Cranston," said Gus, "she's good. Geoff Mercer took a leave of absence to help too. Geoff and Lydia went to Leamington and found your car. Amelia helped Neil while Luke and I came for you."

"Poor Neil," said Suzie, "I've heard tales about Amelia. She's a man-eater. He'll need to watch himself."

"There's a lot of that around," said Gus.

"I don't remember you complaining," said Suzie.

"Do you forgive me," asked Gus, "for the subterfuge, I mean?"

"Of course. You did everything possible to prevent Gardiner and the others from realising you were going ahead with the investigations. If those three get their just desserts, that's good enough for me."

"Your father is outside, waiting patiently," said Gus. "I should go."

"Hold me," said Suzie, "I won't embarrass you by coming out to the Land Rover and making a spectacle of myself."

They kissed.

"I realised something while I was at that house, Gus," Suzie said.

"What was that?" asked Gus.

"I did my best not to fall for you, but I've failed."

"There's a lot of that around too," said Gus, kissing her again.

He left Suzie in the kitchen and walked outside into the moonlit farmyard.

"Everything okay?" asked John Ferris as Gus climbed into the passenger seat.

"It is now," said Gus, "the real fun starts tomorrow."

"Let's get you home," said John Ferris, "there will be time enough for questions another day."

Chapter Seven

Wednesday, 23 May 2018

NEIL AND AMELIA completed the evidence against Culverhouse and Plunkett before they left work on Tuesday evening. Geoff Mercer and Lydia were long gone. There was no sign of Gus returning to the office with Luke, and Alex Hardy was on garden leave.

When they reached the car park, Neil remembered Geoff Mercer had brought Amelia in from Devizes early that morning.

"You need a lift, I guess?" he said, unlocking his car.

"No rush," she replied, "we can stop for a drink. I wouldn't mind grabbing a burger, too; I'm starving."

"Okay, we can run through the presentation one last time. I can't be too late, though; Melody will worry."

Neil dropped Amelia at home an hour and a half later. Melody was asleep when he got home. Neil wondered why he felt guilty; nothing happened. It made a change to relax over a drink and chat with someone from work. Amelia was good company.

Neil rose early the following day. Melody was feeling uncomfortable again; she couldn't settle.

"Why not call the doctor," said Neil, "to put your mind at rest? We've both suffered so much stress of late. It's bound to take its toll."

Melody started to say something, but Neil's mobile rang.

It was Gus Freeman.

"Neil, we got Suzie Ferris back unharmed late last night. Luke drove home alone from the farm. John Ferris brought me back to my bungalow, so my car's still stuck at the office. Can you collect me on your way to work, please?"

"That's terrific news. Okay, guv. No problem. I'm leaving the house now."

Gus rang off, happy he could finish eating his fried breakfast.

"Suzie's safe. I'll get the full story later. Another busy day, darling. I expect I'll be late," said Neil as he kissed Melody goodbye.

His phone rang again. This time it was Amelia Cranston.

"Hi, Neil. Would you like to give me a lift to work?"

"Isn't Geoff Mercer taking you?" asked Neil. "I have to go via Urchfont to pick up Gus. Suzie's home, by the way."

Neil was talking to himself.

Amelia had rung off.

"Who was that?" asked Melody.

"The WPC they landed us with to work on Dad's murder. She stayed on this week too. There was confusion over transport arrangements. It's sorted now."

Neil left the house and drove to Urchfont. He spotted

Gus standing in his driveway, studying the climbing roses on the side of the bungalow.

"They're looking terrific," he said once Gus sat in the passenger seat.

"They're the one remaining thing Tess would be happy about," moaned Gus.

Neil kept his eyes on the road ahead. There were days when he didn't have a clue what his boss was thinking.

"I see Luke Sherman grabbed Alex's parking spot," said Neil when they arrived at the Old Police Station.

"Lydia's here too; that's good to see. Geoff Mercer will need to find a spare bay reserved for the great unwashed to park."

"DS Mercer could be late, guv," said Neil. "He'll be bringing Amelia in, won't he?"

They joined Luke and Lydia upstairs and waited for the others to arrive.

"Luke updated me on yesterday's events, guv," said Lydia, "I'm so pleased Suzie Ferris is OK."

"So am I," said Gus. "How was Alex last night?"

Lydia blushed.

"He's devastated, guv. He knows he let you down."

"Geoff said that Alex tried to get me to review the wall-board earlier in the day, but my head was in the clouds. I need to set things right between us. Alex is a valuable member of the team when he's fully fit. We need to get him back as soon as possible."

The lift arrived, and the doors opened. Amelia breezed in first, followed by a breathless Geoff Mercer.

"Sorry, we're a few minutes late," said Geoff, "I was halfway here before I remembered I needed to collect WPC Cranston. No harm done. We're all present and correct now."

"Apart from Alex, everyone is up to speed regarding Suzie Ferris," said Gus. "When she'll return to work is anyone's guess. I suggest we concentrate on this presentation first and review the original murder file for our latest case. It feels like a lifetime since we worked our last cold case on Friday, but it's still only Wednesday. We can catch up on the two lost days with a concerted effort."

"That works for me," said Geoff, "I reckon we can hang on to Luke until Alex returns to the fold. I'll check that with the ACC, but Amelia may need to resume her normal duties once today's out. If we hang on to her for too long, it will prompt questions from Her Ladyship."

"Over to you then, Neil. Give us the news."

"The Bramshill reunion took place on the twenty-second of September 2012. Sixteen officers checked into two hotels in the Basingstoke area on Saturday. Ten people stayed at Oakley Hall, the venue for the evening's celebrations. Culverhouse and Plunkett were among six officers staying at the Red Lion Hotel in the town. Sandra Plunkett travelled from Lichfield by train. Culverhouse drove from Portishead in his Porsche Boxster 981 Convertible. He bought a new one in 2010. All sixteen officers checked out on Sunday and returned home. A handful hung around for lunch. We collected the names of the attendees from the hotel proprietors. Both were very helpful."

"Have we spoken with the other fourteen officers present?" Geoff Mercer asked.

"Not everybody, Sir," said Neil. "We had problems getting the higher-ranking ones among them to call back. We have their names, confirmation of the bookings and printouts showing their credit card payments. We can hand these details to the Independent Office for Police Conduct.

They shouldn't have any problems getting witness statements. There's no denying they were there."

"What did you learn from the few officers who returned your call?" asked Gus.

"We got confirmation of where they were on Saturday night, how they got there if they travelled to Oakley Hall from Basingstoke. Culverhouse brought Plunkett in the Porsche. A teetotal Chief Superintendent from Surrey carried three colleagues staying at the Red Lion there and back. He was happy to be the designated driver."

"You've confirmed that Culverhouse drove to Oakley Hall," said Gus, "but what about the return journey? Did anyone see them leave for Basingstoke?"

"None of the officers we spoke to could remember exactly, guv. They left together, but when and who drove, they couldn't say. The Chief Super told Luke there were sore heads on Sunday morning. He had his windows open on the drive home to Guildford later in the day because his car still reeked of alcohol. Everybody had a great time, he said."

"Not the victim, Jason Whitworth," said Gus.

"Can we confirm what happened to the Porsche Boxster?" asked Geoff.

"We can do better than that," said Amelia Cranston, "we can show you a photograph taken last August. It's still on the road."

"I don't believe it," said Gus, "surely, Culverhouse got rid of it."

"Oh, he did, guv, or thought he did," said Neil. "Whoever was driving at the time of the accident didn't stop after they hit Jason Whitworth. If they did, it was only for a moment or two. The car was still driveable. They returned to the Red Lion and parked the car near the waste bins."

"How on earth do we know that?" asked Gus.

"They employ a retired postman to do the bottling-up on a Saturday and Sunday morning, guv. He's in his mid-seventies now, but when I mentioned the Boxster, he remembered it. Phil Walker is his name. He was throwing empties into one of those huge commercial bins when he spotted damage to the car's front nearside wing. It was parked right next to the bin. It was so close that Walker wondered if it was where the damage occurred."

"That's interesting," said Gus, "but it doesn't explain why it's still on the road."

"Luke traced the garage where Culverhouse bought it in 2010, and on the off-chance, he asked the Hub to check for the number plate in the ANPR system. He didn't expect to find it, and we were surprised when it turned up in Port Talbot."

"The current owner, Mr Alun Punter, bought it from a garage in Avonmouth," said Amelia. "When I dug deeper, I found the owner had regular run-ins with trading standards before he retired. So if you wanted a new MOT certificate for a car that no reputable garage would let back on the road, it was where you went. He swore blind he'd never heard of Culverhouse or a Porsche Boxster."

"It seems more likely Culverhouse took it to a back-street business and paid the guy to scrap it," said Neil. "Instead, the dodgy dealer repaired it and sold it. We've got Mr Punter's details. Our internal affairs people can check the car over to prove it was involved in an accident."

"So, we can prove those two stayed at the same hotel in Basingstoke," said Geoff. "They travelled together to Oakley Hall and back on Saturday night. The Boxster suffered damage between leaving the Hall and reaching the Red Lion. Nobody mentioned the damage earlier. Phil

Walker can verify the damaged area of the vehicle. That car is now in Port Talbot and will display evidence of that past repair. Do we have enough to pass this on to IOPC?"

"I think we have more than enough to call a halt to their glittering careers," said Gus.

"Are there any holes we've missed?" asked Neil.

"It would help if IOPC interviewed those fourteen officers and someone remembers Culverhouse driving away from Oakley Hall with Sandra Plunkett," said Gus.

"Or, if he was rolling drunk like several others, they saw Sandra Plunkett get behind the wheel," said Geoff.

"Right, Neil, gather everything together," said Gus, "remember what I said before. No digital record. Every scrap of paperwork must get duplicated and filed in separate secure locations."

"Got you, guv," said Neil.

"I'll warn the ACC I'm on my way," said Geoff, "once I've taken him through it, we'll contact the IOPC. They can take it from there."

"What about Ricky Gardiner, guv," asked Luke Sherman.

"I think you and Neil should pass everything we have on Gardiner to DCI Pinnock at Leek Wootton," said Gus.

"Agreed," said Geoff Mercer, "this is a Crime Review Team. Warwickshire Police are running an ongoing investigation into Suzie's kidnapping. They can use what we uncovered to assist their enquiries. I'll ask them to keep me informed of their progress. We must focus this team's attention on the cold case. Gus needs to get back to what he does best."

"As much as it pains me not to go chasing Gardiner around the country," said Gus, "DS Mercer's right. The victim in the next unsolved murder has waited too long for justice. What do we have, Neil?"

"For our next mystery," said Neil, "we've got the murder file for Dennis Gates, a forty-nine-year-old car dealer murdered in Marlborough eight years ago. A possible contract killing. A young man drove onto the garage's forecourt, pulled up by the office door, and calmly walked around the front of the car. Gates came to the door expecting to greet a potential customer, and the killer swung the gun up and fired twice from point-blank range, hitting Gates in the throat."

"Were there any witnesses, Neil?" asked Lydia.

"The attack took place during the school holidays," said Neil, "Gates's fifteen-year-old son, William, spent weekdays in the office with his father because, Annie, his mother owned a mobile dog-grooming business."

"Pampered pets," muttered Lydia.

"Oh, you've heard of them?" asked Neil.

"No, just passing comment," said Lydia.

Gus smiled to himself. They were back in the old routine.

Neil continued to outline the details in the murder file.

"The suspect was described as a white male between twenty-five and forty, medium height and slim with spiky black hair. He wore a dark hooded jacket. The jacket was navy-blue rather than black, and there was a tear in the right knee of his jeans."

"Who described the suspect?" asked Amelia.

"William, the son," said Neil.

"Weren't there any CCTV cameras covering the show-room forecourt?" asked Amelia.

"The images were worse than useless," said Neil, "they contained a rear view of the killer. The images confirmed it was a man and that William's description wasn't miles away from the truth. The torn jeans were so random that they accepted it as the truth. Why bother making it up?"

"The original investigation thought this was a contract killing, is that right?" asked Gus.

"In Marlborough, guv?" asked Luke, "there can't be many contract killers on the streets there."

"In 2010, the Senior Investigating Officer believed ten hitmen were operating in the South of England," said Neil. "As with everything else in life, the more you pay, the better service you get. Prices ranged from a grand to twenty grand."

"How far did they get before they switched their attention to another case?" asked Lydia.

"It was the familiar story," said Neil, "the detectives followed the usual drill. They considered whether the partner, Annie, other family members, or one of their neighbours could be behind the killing. They looked at people who worked for Gates and his business rivals. Gates's bank accounts got checked for any sign of fraud or money laundering. The team used HOLMES to search for links to criminals."

"Nothing turned up in the first two weeks, and it got scaled back," said Geoff Mercer, "the detectives moved on to something new."

"Were you involved in this one, Geoff?" asked Gus.

"Not directly, the Senior Investigating Officer was a chap called Trefor Davies, he transferred into Marlborough ten years ago from Brecon. Very Welsh, loved his rugby and didn't need an excuse to sing whenever I met him on a social occasion."

"I heard his name mentioned," said Gus, "most people described him as being solid."

"From, the neck up, unfortunately," said Geoff, "he hasn't climbed any further. You'll find him in the same station as when he ran that enquiry."

"They reopened the case three years ago," said Neil. "DI Davies commented that the killing left his detectives baffled, but new information meant that a reward was now available for information leading to an arrest."

"What make of car was the killer driving?" asked Luke, "was that caught on camera?"

"The son described it as a red Fiesta," said Neil. "He'd worked with his father long enough to distinguish one make from another. The CCTV image was blurred, but it was a tango red Ford Fiesta. No view of the number plate. From the styling, the best guess at the time was it was a 2006 model."

"More suited to a boy racer than a guy in his thirties or forties," said Gus, "perhaps our killer was closer to the lower end of that age range. Did they have a photo of a twenty-five-year-old hitman to put in front of William Gates?"

"It appeared not," said Neil.

Geoff Mercer had been busy collecting the paperwork he needed.

"I wish you the very best of luck," said Geoff Mercer, "I've got everything. The ACC is waiting by the window of his office, looking for my car to arrive. We'll set the ball rolling this afternoon. Amelia, you had better come back to London Road with me."

"DS Davis can get me home at the end of the day, Sir. I can still be useful."

Gus spotted that Geoff ignored the pout.

Amelia's reputation preceded her.

"No doubt, WPC Cranston," said Geoff, "but your temporary assignment is at an end. I'm sure Mr Freeman will keep a note of your name should he ever need an extra body."

Amelia Cranston knew when to quit. She flounced after Geoff Mercer as he walked to the lift.

"I'm back, Neil," Luke reminded him as the lift descended to the car park. "I'm not as attractive, but I am willing and able."

"In that case, split these names between you and Lydia and start analysing witness statements. I'll dig deeper into the new information that surfaced."

"Before you get stuck into that, Lydia," said Gus. "What was the name of the officer who worked with DS Mercer in Leamington?"

"DI Andy Carlton, guv," she replied.

"I wonder if he's heard the news about Suzie. I'll call him. He might have an idea when they'll release her car."

"Have you heard from Suzie this morning, guv?" asked Lydia.

"No, I doubt if she slept well last night. When her father drove me home last night, he said they would call the family doctor this morning. The medics at Leek Wootton tended to her physical wounds, but Suzie may need a different kind of help in the coming weeks."

"Give her our love when you see her next," said Lydia.

Gus wondered when that might be. There were so many demands on his time. He knew that handing the hunt for Ricky Gardiner over to Leek Wootton was the right move. As regards the hit-and-run case, he could rely on the IOPC to act with due diligence. The new organisation had the power now to initiate investigations without relying on a force to record and refer a complaint or accusation of misconduct.

Those two matters were now in someone else's hands,

and yet Gus couldn't help wanting to keep tabs on their progress. The new case looked to have interesting aspects. They might discover the killer in due course, and this time Gus hoped their work resulted in the guilty party facing trial.

As for matters closer to home, he needed to visit Alex and apologise for his outburst. There were no shortcuts to total recovery from a severe accident. Gus suspected Alex was attempting to find one.

The team had Terry Davis's funeral to attend next week. That would be an emotional occasion, and Carole Brown would soon finalise arrangements for Tony's funeral. Gus thought what a pleasant change an invitation to a wedding or a christening would make to break the cycle?

Then there were affairs of the heart. Gus had never looked at another woman during forty years of marriage. How did he get into such a mess within three years of Tess's death? Vera was an attractive, warm and intelligent woman only a handful of years younger than himself. She deserved to find happiness after the collapse of her marriage. They were good together.

The last thing Gus wanted to do was hurt Vera, but it was inevitable when the truth came out about Suzie Ferris. At first, he had regarded the Bank Holiday weekend as an aberration due to Suzie being drunk and upset. He thought she would realise a relationship with a man old enough to be her father was out of the question. Gus hoped to let her down gently, and they could agree to remain friends.

The kidnapping changed that. When John Ferris rang him on Sunday evening, he started to worry. By Monday morning and Gardiner's chilling message, he was desperate. Now he realised he was as smitten as Suzie. There's no fool like an old fool.

Gus glanced across at Neil, Lydia and Luke. They were engrossed in the Gates case. He wondered whether they would miss him if he took the afternoon off after he'd called DI Carlton. He could only think of one spot where these different demands on his time could receive careful consideration and get resolved. Gus was heading for his allotment in Urchfont.

Thursday, 24 May 2018

"WELCOME BACK, GUV," said Neil, "did you enjoy the break?"

"I didn't think you'd miss me, Neil."

"We didn't stay as late as on previous nights, I grant you, but we've compiled a list of witnesses to re-interview. I took a closer look at the new evidence. Do you want to go through it with me?"

"What will Luke and Lydia be doing when they arrive?" asked Gus.

"Contacting our witnesses to arrange times and dates, guv," said Neil, "they'll have enough to occupy them until lunchtime."

"Set them up on that when they get here, Neil. First, I'll skim through the reports in the murder file, then when you're free; we'll go over our first impressions. Does that make sense?"

Neil nodded and dumped the thick murder file on Gus's desk.

Gus started to read three-year-old media reports.

'Detectives swooped on garages across the West to make arrests. The majority were in the Swindon area.

Police discovered a gang buying second-hand cars from auctions and then significantly reducing the mileage and getting new documents for the vehicles before selling them. Detective Inspector Trefor Davies told this reporter: "It's been a productive and lengthy investigation involving a huge volume of paperwork and documents. The operation was one of the largest that Wiltshire Police has ever undertaken. It will be harder for this to happen again because we will be alive to it and be ready to support our partners in immediate investigations. This case sends out a clear message that you can't get away with this sort of crime. It is also a timely moment to remind people that when you buy a car, make sure you get its complete history and documentation. That helps us prevent scams such as this reoccurring.'

'Detectives believe one-hundred and fifty cars were involved in the clocking scam that involved vehicles worth three-quarters of a million pounds. Operation Loki saw officers seize logbooks, MOT details, financial documents and computers from eleven garages.'

Fascinating stuff, Gus thought, but how does this connect to the Gates case?

Neil was free now. Luke and Lydia were busy phoning potential witnesses.

"I thought clocking was an ancient analogue crime, Neil," he said, "why didn't this disappear when everything went digital?"

"Electronic displays can leave motorists more vulnerable behind the wheel than ever, guv. According to the latest figures, the number of cars on UK roads with mileage discrepancies has risen to over five per cent. The number of vehicles clocked has shot up, with an increase of nearly a third in just five years."

"A lucrative business, I imagine. With the already belea-guered motorist out of pocket."

"To the tune of eight hundred million pounds, guv."

Gus whistled.

"Walk me through the rest of this, Neil," said Gus, "my Ford Focus has never had any mileage adjustments. I think it resembles a dying breed of human. One which grows old gracefully."

"Clocking is easier for newer cars because they don't get MOT tested for the first three or four years. With no official record of their mileage, it's difficult to verify. It can be almost impossible to tell a clocked vehicle just by looking at it, which makes a vehicle history check a vital form of protection for buyers. A clocked vehicle could hide dangerous levels of wear and tear depending on a private owner's profession."

"So Trefor Davies and his team found a gang systemati-cally fiddling the odometers on hundreds of cars," said Gus, "where's the link to Gates's murder five years earlier?"

"One of the cars was a tango red Ford Fiesta, registered in 2006, with a mileage that suggested it had one lady-owner who used it to do her weekly shop."

"If Trefor Davies found the killer's car, how come they didn't make an arrest? Surely, it couldn't be hard to trace the owner?"

"If only it were that simple, guv," said Neil. "I reckon I know the problem they faced."

"Enlighten me," sighed Gus.

"You could be right about the gunman's age. Have you heard the term company car?"

"Of course, but as far as I remember, they tend to be driven into the ground by sales reps. The majority of whom are gainfully employed."

"Teenage gangs often have a car available for anyone to use. These cars usually don't last long. This Fiesta either led a charmed life, or it acquired a sentimental value over the years. Cars get stolen day in and day out by kids, as you know. The thieves can range from twelve years and over. The younger ones can't hold a driving licence, and the older ones often lose theirs due to driving offences. Road tax and insurance are a mystery to them. They're things that only apply to other people. The company car gets parked on a large estate somewhere, and the gang's What's App group spreads the word. One guy uses it to rob a convenience store and returns it. Another guy borrows it to facilitate his drug deals. If things get hairy and the police chase a young tearaway, he dumps the car and sets it alight. No worries, there's always another car to take its place sitting on a driveway asking to get nicked."

"So, this Fiesta lingered in the Swindon area for five years?" said Gus, "is that likely?"

"There's little doubt it was the same car, guv," said Neil. "If we hunt through the appendices to this murder file, we'll find a forensic report. I bet they found a thousand smudged fingerprints. The task of tying one of those to the guy in that blurred CCTV image would be a nightmare. I guess that's why they offered a reward. It was a last throw of the dice to entice a past gang member to give up a name. Big surprise. They got no takers, and Trefor Davies tucked the reward money away for a rainy day."

"Is there any point finding out who the rightful owner was of the Fiesta back in 2006?" asked Gus. "I know it may be a daft question, but was there a logbook? Did the DVLA get notification of transfer of ownership between 2006 and the day of the murder in 2010?"

"We can double-check that, guv," said Neil, "although it

may lie deeper in this file. There are reams of it to plough through yet. If I'm right and it got stolen, when was it taken? Did the killer nick it that day because he had a contract to carry out? If so, why didn't he just get rid of it within hours of the hit?"

"If he was a youngster, as I surmised, Gates could have been his first kill. Perhaps he was too thick to realise there were CCTV cameras at the garage. Did he know William Gates was in the showroom during the summer holidays? Our killer sounds more and more amateur, Neil. What did he do with the car after he left the garage, I wonder?"

"If only the car hadn't got clocked, guv. If the car was in regular use from new, we should know what the mileage would be, but how far did they rewind it? Also, what if this killer stashed the Fiesta in his grannie's garage for a couple of years? Anything could have happened."

"Names, Neil, that's our starting point," said Gus, "fix a meeting with DI Trefor Davies. We need the names of teenage gang members active in the Marlborough and Swindon area eight years ago. He'll still be familiar with many of them. Then I want Lydia and Luke to scour social media for photographs of these characters with the car. That Fiesta was still a flash piece of kit eight years ago. Whoever drove it couldn't resist posting a picture of it sat on their driveway or the front at Weymouth. We must narrow the search."

Neil left to make the call. Gus continued to trawl through the murder file.

He found a newspaper report of the murder.

Neighbours spoke of their shock today after an ordinary father was shot dead outside his garage in a suspected gangland hit. Dennis Gates, forty-nine, was shot twice in the neck. Paramedics fought for thirty minutes to resuscitate the victim as he lay motionless on the forecourt.

The victim's family home sits on a leafy lane opposite the local Golf Club. The car dealer moved into the detached five-bedroom house in Shelton Lane last July. His partner, Annie, 47, was secretary of the local football team and known as a popular mum.

One neighbour said: 'We can't believe it. I thought they were just an ordinary family. Annie volunteered at the local football club, and the boy was always smiling. You'd see them leaving the house together at the weekends.'

Another mum said: "You never heard anything out of the ordinary about them. I just saw his stylish car and thought he must be a successful businessman. Now we're terrified. My kids couldn't sleep last night."

"Annie is a smashing lady and has been helping us for the last few years in her spare time," Mick Judge, chairman of the local club, told this reporter. "She's a real football fanatic, with her son playing at the club, and she comes to every match. I'd never thought her partner was involved in anything dodgy. I met him at a social event last year, and everything seemed okay. Nothing felt off about him. He was a friendly guy who came to football matches. I'm shocked."

"Annie and her family were shocked and devastated by Dennis's death," Annie's younger sister, Sarah, said, "Dennis was an only child; he never spoke about his parents much. I'm not sure if they're still alive. We are devastated and in shock. Dennis was a loving father, and he was always there for Annie and their son. He looked out for everyone. He was a happy guy, always laughing."

Detectives are investigating theories that Gates was the victim of a long-running gangland feud. They are hunting a lone gunman who fired two shots before driving away towards Poulton Hill.

Detective Chief Inspector Trefor Davies, leading the murder inquiry, said: "At this stage, everything indicates this was a targeted act and not in any way random. I can assure anyone who assists officers by providing information we will treat any contact they make in the strictest of confidence."

There was more of the same over the next few weeks until the investigation faltered. Three years ago, Trefor Davies made sure every local paper featured his appeal for further information. Nobody could accuse Trefor Davies of not being thorough.

Gus wondered whether that was the problem in this case.

They gathered so much data they forgot to ask the simple questions.

If this was a contract killing, who issued the contract and why?

Why had a respectable garage owner and family man deserved to die?

Chapter Eight

"I'M UP TO SPEED NOW," said Gus, "what have you three achieved in the past two hours?"

"You can meet with Trefor Davies in the morning, guv," said Neil, "he's expecting you at nine-thirty."

"I'll drive straight there from Urchfont," said Gus. He rubbed his hands. He could have a lie-in tomorrow, as it was only a thirty-minute drive through Upavon and Pewsey to reach Marlborough.

"Don't you need one of us to go with you, guv?" asked Lydia.

"Drat, I was forgetting. Neil, you're driving us. Pick me up at nine."

"No problem, guv," said Neil.

"I've got more details on Annie and her son, William," said Luke.

"Any interview times fixed yet?"

"Annie's busy with her mobile dog-grooming appointments. She suggested five o'clock tomorrow afternoon. William will be home then."

"He doesn't need a responsible adult," said Gus, "William was fifteen when his father died. The lad's twenty-three now. I'd prefer to see them alone. There's nothing to show the wife had anything to do with her husband's death, but William may have known the gunman."

"You don't think he was involved, guv, surely?" asked Lydia.

"When Neil and I mulled over the evidence in the murder file, I became more convinced the killer was under twenty-five. The car he drove, the clothing we saw on the CCTV, points to a younger man. The killer's method smacks of an amateur with a handgun. Then there's what he did with the car afterwards, or what he didn't do—any professional ditches the car within hours. Where the police got this gangland feud idea from, I can't imagine. There's nothing to support it in the file. My meeting with Trefor Davies in the morning might explain matters. If he produces a solid link between Gates and the criminal under-world, then I'll have egg on my face, and we'll start anew."

"So, you think William Gates knew the killer because they'd come into contact through school, sport or just hanging out?" asked Lydia.

"If the killer was a teenager, why not? Think of the description we received; he was a white male of medium height and slim with spiky black hair. He wore a dark hooded jacket. Killers come in all shapes and sizes, I know, but that description described ninety per cent of teenage boys eight years ago. Recheck the CCTV. Was he a sagger?"

"Get you, guv," said Lydia, "if he was, he was not cool. That went out of fashion by the early Noughties."

"No, guv," said Luke, "I agree with Lydia. That blurred image we saw didn't help us discern the guy's age with any accuracy, but those jeans looked the right style for the time. My guess is they were a faded pair of denim jeans with original rips. The material hadn't got damaged by rough treatment."

"I try to keep up with the trends," said Gus. "I might be five years off track with my stab in the dark, but do you accept William and the killer may have met?"

"It's possible," said Neil, "so it makes sense to talk to the mother and son separately."

"Luke, you and Lydia visit Gates's partner, Annie, tomorrow afternoon. Neil and I will arrange a time to speak to William earlier in the day. We should finish with DI Davies by eleven o'clock. Where does William work?"

"At the garage, guv," said Luke, "Annie got a manager in for a few years, and William worked there at weekends and during the holidays. When he turned eighteen, he went full time, and after a year, the manager left. William has run the place alone for four years."

"I don't suppose the Gates's garage was on the list from three years ago?" asked Gus.

"The clocking gang, guv," asked Neil, "no chance."

"Don't worry, Neil. I'm not trying to fit him up. I'm shuffling my pieces of the jigsaw around until I get some to interlock. If that wasn't the garage containing the tango red Fiesta, we might need to visit the one that did. I want to see who worked there, what sort of place it is. That's another job to add to our list for tomorrow, Neil. No point dropping by, though, until we've got a list of names from Trefor Davies."

"Is there anything else I can do for you this afternoon, guv?" asked Lydia.

"I'll shout a few facts and figures, Lydia. Scribble them on a whiteboard."

Lydia walked across to the nearest board and stood poised with her marker pen.

"Don't go too quick, guv,"

"Annie Frayling, born in 1963. Educated at St Mary's Primary school and the local comprehensive until St John's opened in 1975. The comprehensive merged with the Royal Free school in that year. She left school at sixteen and worked at a supermarket, a hairdresser's and dog kennels. Annie moved in with Dennis Gates in 1993. William was born in 1995."

"What about Dennis Gates?" asked Lydia.

"He was born in 1961," said Neil, "it stands to reason. Gates was forty-nine when he died."

"Don't write for a second, Lydia," said Gus, "here we go. Sarah, Annie's sister, said he was an only child. Dennis never mentioned his parents, so the family assumed they were dead. We'll dig deeper when we speak with Annie; to get his place of birth, where he went to school, and what jobs he had before arriving in Marlborough in the early Nineties."

"I've made a note of that, guv," said Neil. "any link to a criminal element could lie hidden way back and relate to his life before he met Annie."

"It explains why he kept it from Annie and her family," added Luke, "there was no mention of a criminal record in DI Davies's murder file, though, was there?"

"I should hope that they checked," said Gus, "it's basic. I hate going over the same ground too much with these cold cases. We should find new witnesses or at least new questions to ask the original suspects. It doesn't feel right checking the investigation step-by-step, hoping to find they made mistakes."

"I'll ask the Hub for information on Dennis Gates, guv,"

said Neil, "Luke can chase it up tomorrow morning while we're in Marlborough."

"Have you done with the whiteboard, for now, guv?" asked Lydia.

While Gus thought about what else they needed, Luke chipped in.

"Can you fill in the detail between when they got together and Dennis's death, guv?" he asked.

"Was Gates a garage owner throughout his working life?" asked Lydia.

"Pass," said Gus, "we don't have enough on him yet. Annie worked in a beauty salon until William was born. Gates must have been doing okay because she stayed at home until the lad started school. Then soon after, Annie set up this dog-grooming business of hers. Gates furnished her with a van, converted it to accommodate her equipment, and Annie went mobile in 2000. William showed an aptitude for football. He was never good enough for a professional standard, but the local club had him on their books from nine years old. Annie became a familiar face on the touchline and gravitated to the club secretary by 2006. Dennis and Annie were both successful in their businesses, and the family moved to Shelton Lane in July 2009. The new home was a five-bedroomed detached house, and before that, they lived in a three-bedroomed semi-detached property close to St Mary's Primary school."

"We can check when Gates took over the garage showroom, guv," said Luke.

"Do that, Luke," said Gus, "Gates was thirty when he moved to Marlborough. That's a reasonable age to get established in your chosen career. I can't see any argument with that. It doesn't appear he bought his way into a successful business with the money he got from a life of crime. Everyone who knew Dennis said he was a good father, a good partner, always friendly and always smiling."

"Which is why we keep wondering why someone shot him," said Lydia.

"When I took the first pass through that murder file with Amelia, it struck me that the Gates's life was too good to be true," said Neil.

"I've told you before, Neil," said Gus, "you're far too cynical for one so young. That scepticism over a family living in perfect harmony usually arrives when you're my age."

"I blame my father," said Neil, "he never accepted things at face value. If you see someone walking around with a permanent smile on their face, they're hiding something. That's what he reckoned. Either they know something you don't know, he'd say, or when the mask slips, you'd see they were falling apart inside."

"Anything could cause that," said Lydia, "domestic abuse is top of the list, money troubles, a drink or drug problem, or another brand of pressure."

"Carry on, Lydia," said Gus, "what are you thinking?"

"What if there *was* a gangland connection, guv? Something from his past, before Dennis Gates arrived in Marlborough. Maybe his past caught up with him. Someone was putting the squeeze on him, something similar to the clocking racket Wiltshire Police uncovered five years later. Who's to say that it didn't start earlier?"

"Write that on the wallboard somewhere, Lydia. It's a theory worth pursuing. That's something we can discuss with Trefor Davies in the morning."

"When I look at that murder file and compare it to the other cases we've investigated, it seems to contain so much, and yet it still feels incomplete," said Neil. "As if the data collection was random and haphazard. I can't see a structure."

"Murder cases have a particular arrangement of events, Neil," said Gus. "Not just the order in which they occurred, but in their significance. The first twenty-four hours is critical. Certain types of evidence fade, so they get collected first. Was that evidence of any significance in this case? With hindsight, we might decide not, but sometimes we can arrest the culprit during that period even with a minimum amount of evidence. If we do then almost always, it leads to a successful conviction."

"I wonder when DI Davies started to imagine it was a contract killing?" said Lydia.

"How the gunman arrived on the forecourt may have triggered that," said Luke. "He drove in, got out of the car and walked straight towards Gates. There was no argument, no demand for money, no words spoken. Just two shots in the throat, and then the killer drove away."

"Why the throat?" asked Lydia, "was that to send a message to others not to talk?"

"The police found no evidence to suggest problems between Gates and any of his business rivals or his friends," said Gus, "don't lose sight of the time frame. The first twenty-four hours had passed, and they had days to wait for forensic results to surface. William was the only eyewitness. The CCTV footage was next to useless. If they identified a suspect at that time, they had nothing to put in front of them. Something the suspect couldn't dispute. We've seen from the cold cases passed to us that not only did the one-week milestone get reached, but several weeks elapsed before they called off the hunt. Even as they entered week two, the team would start to doubt whether a successful outcome was possible. DI Davies hoped forensics would supply a magic bullet. It never materialised. His team of detectives scrolled through lists hoping to find a match. A way to link a name on the screen to the events they pieced together. Trefor Davies will tell us what other pressing crime raised its head to persuade their superiors it was time to call it quits."

"We're closing in on the first twenty-four hours, guv, of our investigation," said Neil, "and I can't see we've made any progress. It's still a mystery."

"We're not as concerned with the clock as Trefor Davies was," said Gus, "we can take as long as we need. Let's see where we stand at the close of play tomorrow."

Although the clock wasn't their enemy, it still ticked around to five o'clock.

Lydia dashed to Alex's home to check on his welfare.

Luke drove into town for shopping. He and Nicky had a party to attend on Saturday evening. They couldn't arrive without a gift and a good bottle of wine.

When Neil arrived home, he found Melody on the settee, wrapped in her dressing gown. She looked thoroughly miserable.

"Did you call the doctor?" he asked as he placed a cooling hand on her forehead.

"It doesn't feel right, Neil," she said.

"You mean the baby?"

Melody nodded. Neil rang his mother. Ten minutes later, Neil and Melody were in the car and heading for the hospital.

While his team spent their evening in different ways, Gus trod a familiar path. He stopped off at the allotment to catch Bert Penman before he disappeared. It was a busy time for gardeners, and Gus felt guilty, leaving Bert with a double-helping of late.

They spent thirty minutes catching up on Bert's progress, and Gus made a list of things he could help with over the weekend. He needed to do his share. Gus kept his fingers crossed that nothing cropped up to interfere with his plans.

When he reached the bungalow, he called Suzie.

John Ferris answered.

"Hello, John, Suzie not there?"

"The doctor gave her something to help her sleep. She was awake most of last night."

"I'm not surprised," said Gus, "it will take time to get back on an even keel. Tell her I called, won't you?"

"Of course, Gus," said John, "the doctor signed her off until the end of next week."

"I can rely on you and Jackie to make sure she doesn't try to go back too soon."

"I'll get Suzie to give you a call tomorrow, Gus."

"Thanks, John. We're in Marlborough for most of the day. I won't get home until six at the earliest. Any time after that will be fine."

Gus wandered into the kitchen to prepare his evening meal. After a hectic few days, he looked forward to an evening with a book, a glass of red wine and a decent album playing in the background.

Neil Davis called him a few minutes before eleven. Gus was slipping a precious vinyl album into its protective cover and getting ready to head for his bed.

"Sorry to call so late, guv," said Neil.

"Not to worry, I was still awake. It must be important, so what's the problem?"

"I've just got back from the hospital. We lost the baby, guv. Melody was feeling low this morning. I should have listened to her. I got distracted and didn't realise how much discomfort she was suffering. She laid around all day, fretting, and as soon as I saw her when I got home, I knew we should have done something sooner. They're keeping her in overnight. I won't be able to make it in the morning, guv. Do you want me to call Luke?"

"I'll call Luke, Neil. I'm so sorry," said Gus.

"It's just one thing after the other at the minute," said Neil. "I don't know what's happening next, but if I don't see you before, I'll see you on Thursday at the crematorium."

Neil ended the call. Gus stood in the lounge, holding the phone for several minutes. A few short weeks ago, the Crime Review Team was a happy band with everything they touched turning to gold.

How fickle life could be? There were two tragedies in the Davis family in quick succession and Alex Hardy coping with his physical and mental wellbeing. Lydia's concern for her colleague meant her concentration had to be affected. Gus prayed Luke remained unscathed.

As for himself, the battle to bring Culverhouse and Plunkett to book for their devious dealings should draw to a successful conclusion within days. Unless there was another stumbling block lying in wait around the corner. Ricky Gardiner was still at large, and Gus wouldn't relax until he was caught and charged with murder and kidnapping.

Suzie Ferris was back in the bosom of her family, and in time she'd resume work at London Road. Of course, questions would be asked, and Gus knew it was only a matter of time before Vera put two and two together.

There was no relief. Each member of their original band of four was in a dark place with no immediate signs of improvement.

Gus elected to send Luke a brief text asking him to pick him up at nine o'clock. He could explain the reason for

Neil's absence face-to-face in the morning. Gus made a note to call Lydia before they left for Marlborough. She would have to carry on in the office on her own. As he trudged through to his bedroom, Gus remembered how much he'd anticipated a quiet evening at home. Right now, the last thing he wanted was to spend the night alone.

Friday, 25 May 2018

"GOOD MORNING, GUV," said Luke when Gus answered the door.

"Sorry, Luke. I overslept," said Gus. "Neil called me late last night to say Melody suffered a miscarriage."

"Nicky wondered why you sent the late text. I only read it at seven-thirty this morning. Oh, what dreadful news. At sixteen weeks too," said Luke, "okay, they only saw the baby on an ultrasound, but they still formed a bond, especially Melody. Neil moaned about the morning sickness and the constant baby talk, but he was looking forward to fatherhood."

"Let's get in the car and set off for our first interview of the day," said Gus, "Lydia should be in the office by now. I'll tell her the news. She'll not have anyone else working there today."

"There's plenty to occupy her, guv. Lydia can annoy the Hub people until they provide the lists Neil and I asked them to get."

"Good idea, I hate to think of her twiddling her thumbs," said Gus.

"Upavon and then Pewsey, guv, is that the best route?" asked Luke.

"There are few options, Luke, and Trefor Davies is at the old police station in George Lane, complete with its secure cells built to hold suspect terrorists. The building used to be a children's centre. No doubt they wished they had the secure cells when the rowdier kids were on site. Trefor will retire next year, I expect. The officers left behind are moving to a smaller unit near the town centre."

"I read about that somewhere, guv," said Luke, "the present building will get sold. The local Council needs premises for a doctor's surgery, but the car parking is limited and on an incline which doesn't make it that attractive."

"Let's hope there's a spare spot available this morning, Luke. I don't mind the occasional incline these days. It's walking half a mile from the nearest pay-and-display car park that annoys me."

Thirty minutes later, they turned off George Lane into the car park. There was nothing to suggest the police station was on its last legs. Gus thought the Sixties' styling of red brick and lots of glass was wearing its age pretty well.

Luke grabbed the parking space nearest the door, and at twenty-nine minutes past nine, they negotiated the Reception area and found themselves in DI Trefor Davies's office.

"Thanks for seeing us this morning, Trefor," said Gus, "my colleague DS Davis told you why we were keen to meet with you, I hope?"

"I'm pleased to meet you," said Trefor Davies, "I heard such a lot about you when you worked in Salisbury. This is DS Davis, is it? Good morning."

"No, Sir," said Luke, "I'm DS Luke Sherman, DS Davies couldn't make it."

"I understand you are reviewing the murder of Dennis Gates," said the Welshman, "a nasty business that, and another crime that slipped through without us finding the culprit."

"Perhaps you can talk us through your thinking on the day of the murder, Trefor," said Gus. "We've got the case file. It's comprehensive, isn't it? I'm interested in how you approached it."

"I never met the deceased," said Trefor, "but many of my officers were familiar with the name. He was a solid, upright citizen in their book. In the early Nineties, Dennis Gates moved into the town, settled down with a local girl, and had just the one child, a boy. All three were well known and respected in the community—the sporting community in particular. The lad, William, took after his father and loved his football. The skill he showed as a schoolboy was meaningless when he didn't shoot up in height as so many do these days. No professional club would entertain taking him on when they can sign giants from foreign clubs. When Annie Frayling wasn't at the football club watching her boy or working in the office, she became a familiar sight trundling around town in her old van. She still visits my house every couple of months to give my wife's two Jack Russell's a shampoo. Annie always has a smile on her face, is wonderful with the dogs and just at ease with the customers. Dennis was the same. We never heard a word said against him. The police have had their issues with garages, as you know. We never heard a squeak from anyone who was a customer of Dennis. He was a rare breed, a genuine second-hand car dealer. He was always prepared to go the extra mile to make sure the customer was happy with their choice. You can tell from the murder file he was proud of his boy. Dennis helped support the football club by donating the match ball. There's a newspaper clip in that file some- where. On the day of the shooting, I was in the Town Hall attending yet another boring meeting. When the news broke, nobody could understand it. There were people from all levels of society in attendance. Everyone had a story to tell about Dennis, and without exception, they thought Dennis Gates was the salt of the earth. I felt the eyes of the whole room on me as I left to make my way over to the showroom. I could tell they expected me to find the killer. When I arrived, young William was distraught, as you can imagine. The paramedics were still trying their best to revive Dennis, but it was hopeless. My first thought was it was a robbery. Then, later in the afternoon, I became convinced it was drugs. The gunman had to be high as a kite and wanted cash for his next hit. There were no other possible motives."

"What did you make of William's description of the attacker?" asked Gus.

"It could match with many of the trouble-makers we had in the town. It was vague but convincing. I never doubted William's account of events. Why?"

"I wondered whether he knew the killer, and his vague but plausible description aimed to confuse matters."

"We're back to motive again," said Trefor, "why would William try to confuse us? He would have named his father's killer if he'd known him, surely? When we opened the investigation, we pencilled in two possible scenarios. An attempted robbery where the young attacker panicked and shot Dennis Gates. Or the act of a desperate junkie prepared to kill someone for the cost of a fix."

"What made you switch your focus to a gangland hit?" asked Luke, "there was no explanation of that in the murder file."

"We closed a sizeable cannabis factory on a nearby trading estate earlier in the year. We've suffered our fair share of county lines gangs drifting through the town searching for vulnerable homes. From what I recall from the 2014 report, over one hundred families fell into the vulnerable category. We didn't arrest anyone connected to organised crime, but there was no question they were active here. Some things didn't add up in Gates's history when we checked. He might have left his former home before the police caught up with him. None of that fitted the character of the person everyone thought they knew here in Marlborough. It was a possible motive, without real substance. The media grabbed it as a lifeline. The public wasn't comfortable thinking one of their own murdered such a popular bloke. If they could paint the picture that Gates crossed a London gang in the past and it was they who murdered him, all well and good."

"So, you found discrepancies in Gates's history?" asked Gus.

"I would call them gaps rather than discrepancies," said Trefor, "Dennis was illegitimate. His teenage mother gave him up at birth, and he lived the first three years of his life in a children's home in Ventnor, Isle of Wight. He was adopted by a couple from Hastings in Sussex in the autumn of 1964. Dennis attended schools in the city until he was sixteen. He worked at various garages in Brighton, Eastbourne and Hastings. Then, in the late Eighties, Gates set up business in Newbury, trading as Thornford Motors. Three years later, he bought the premises in Marlborough and began dating Annie Frayling within a few months. They moved in together eighteen months later."

"The gaps appeared where?" asked Gus.

"We traced the garages along the south coast, but Gates left a second-hand car dealer's garage in Eastbourne in 1982, and for the following six years, we found no trace of him on these shores. His last place of employment went bust in the early Noughties, so there was no way of checking the facts, but when local police asked around, they heard the rumour that Dennis flew south. He'd had enough of the rat race and moved to Menorca in the Balearics. Where Gates worked over there, we have no idea. Perhaps he went the full Monty, and dropped out, lived the hippy life, only accepting cash jobs to keep him in food and drink. He turned up again in Hastings not long after his mother died. How he got here? Again, we don't know. Dennis was the only beneficiary of her will. His adoptive father died three years earlier."

"What year did the adoptive mother die?" asked Luke.

"I can't recall the exact date, but it was the late Eighties, probably 1988. We reckoned the windfall financed the Thornford Motors business. He never looked back."

"During your investigation, you questioned the likelihood of a steady, hard-working individual dropping out and disappearing for half a dozen years," said Gus.

DI Trefor Davies nodded.

"It flew in the face of everything we knew of Gates since he moved to Marlborough. We reckoned he was up to no good during that period. He did something that upset people with long memories. It took them over twenty years, but eventually, they found him and settled the score."

"Gates had no criminal record, though," said Luke.

"I could fill a book with the names of crooks that haven't got a record, son," said Trefor Davies, "that's because they never get caught."

"We need to dig deeper into the period between 1982 and 1988," said Gus. "If it was gang-related, then we won't find anyone willing to speak to us. The Menorca angle could be a red-herring too. I wonder who started those rumours in Eastbourne? Let's leave that for now; the first angle sounds like a hopeless task. The second will be time-consuming. Trefor, you're confident William Gates didn't know his father's attacker? OK, does that mean it wasn't a local lad? One thing we know, thanks to your swoop on the clocking gang three years ago, the tango red Fiesta stayed local. Can you supply us with names of the likely lads operating in Marlborough at the time and those who crossed your radar when you had cases in town that got attributed to young Swindon criminals?"

"I can look up several Marlborough names," said Trefor. "Swindon produced such a large number you need to narrow the field. Even so, it might take days to go through my files. What age range are you concentrating on?"

"Eighteen to twenty-five," said Gus.

"Mmm, that doesn't narrow it much, but if I start with the ones with a propensity to violence, that will be more useful."

"What a musical turn of phrase," said Gus, "a propensity to violence. It sounds tailor-made for the Welsh accent. Before you burst into song, can you at least give me the local lads names?"

"The Pearce brothers, Grenville and Gordon. Mick Craddock, Ben Smith and Josh Raymond. All of them have form. They were in and out of trouble from the age of ten onwards. They've served custodial sentences over the years."

"How old were they at the time of the murder?" asked Luke.

"Between twenty and twenty-five," replied Trefor. "Three of them are in prison as we speak, Grenville Pearce and Ben Smith are enjoying a spell of freedom at present. How long it will last, I couldn't say."

"I'd appreciate the details of the Swindon-based crews as soon as you can compile it, Trefor," said Gus Freeman, "but for now, we'll let you get on with your day. Many thanks for your insights into the case. It's been useful."

Trefor Davies stood and walked around his desk to shake the two detectives by the hand.

"I hope you have more luck finding Gates's killer than we did, Gus," he said, "the whole thing appeared so random. There was no rhyme nor reason for it."

"There's always a reason, Trefor," said Gus. "The way we ran murder cases a decade ago and the pressure applied by our superiors to come up with instant answers wasn't conducive to a successful outcome. However, the same constraints don't hamstring my Crime Review Team. We can look at that missing six-year period and scratch beneath the surface of Gate's life. The motive for the killing is there, somewhere."

"That's one of the niggles for which you were famous, I suppose," said Trefor with a wry smile. "A pity that you and I didn't work together back then. I would sleep better at nights with the extra wins I'd have on my record when I retire."

"Those niggles weren't always right, Trefor," said Gus, "but they often started me on a road that led me to the right answer. Others assumed I knew where I was heading all along. Over the years, I thought it better for the villains to believe I was infallible than to inform my superiors they were mistaken."

"That's a line I'll try to remember, Gus," said Trefor Davies, "you've cheered me up no end this morning."

Chapter Nine

GUS AND LUKE left the DI's office and returned to the car park.

"A chink of light in the investigation, guv," said Luke, "that gap in Gates's history has to be significant."

"We'll see, Luke," said Gus, "let's find this garage the son William is running these days. We don't have an appointment, but I want to catch him off-guard."

"You're still not convinced, are you, guv?"

"I don't believe he killed his father, Luke, but something doesn't ring true."

"The garage is on London Road, guv, a five-minute drive," said Luke.

The forecourt and showroom looked prosperous. Luke pulled up beside a top-of-the-range Mercedes.

"I think the Mercedes belongs to the owner," he said, nodding at the WFG 150 number plate.

Gus was unimpressed. He got out of the car and strolled to the large plate-glass window. Gus turned and studied the approach road and the forecourt. Dennis Gates's body fell here. Right next to the entrance door. The killer's tango red Ford Fiesta would have been three yards ahead, parked at a slight angle where the attacker abandoned it. Then he leapt out, walked around the front of the car and...

"Can I help you?"

Gus turned towards the door. A stocky, handsome young man glared up at him with piercing blue eyes and dark, slicked-back hair. This must be William. The well-groomed garage owner wore a suit that would cost Gus a month's wages. Business must be excellent.

"William Gates?" asked Gus.

"William Frayling-Gates. Who wants to know?"

"The name is Freeman," said Gus, "I'm a consultant with Wiltshire Police. Here's my card. We're taking a fresh look into your father's murder. My colleague is DS Sherman. We can't wait around until five o'clock this afternoon to interview you. You're old enough to cope without your mother holding your hand. Shall we find somewhere private? We wouldn't want to scare away your customers, would we?"

"I've nothing to add to the statement I gave eight years ago," said William, "do I need a solicitor?"

"I don't know, do you?" asked Gus, "let's have an informal chat first, and then you can consider your options."

William turned on his heel and strode towards the rear of the showroom. His office lay in the far corner. Luke studied the layout as he followed the garage owner and his boss. The difference in height between the two men was more noticeable now. Frayling-Gates stood five feet nothing, even with the raised heels on his stylish Italian shoes.

Once the three men sat inside the office with the door shut, William appeared more in control. Gus thought the large desk he now had between him and the two nasty police officers did the trick.

"Why are you dragging this up again?" said Frayling-Gates, "my mother doesn't need this. It's taken her years to come to terms with Dad's death. You have no idea."

"Oh, I think we do, Mr Frayling-Gates," said Gus, "we touch base with death regularly. Hardly a day goes by when we don't have to examine someone's life in forensic detail to discover why they got torn from their loved ones in such a cruel fashion. As for this case, our superiors selected it for review. A fresh look at the evidence with no time pressures. We can take as long as we feel necessary to uncover the truth. Let's start with the events of the day in question."

"I told you, I've nothing to add."

"Let me stop you there," said Gus, "looking at your watch every thirty seconds won't make this go any quicker. If you can't co-operate with us in the comfort of your office, I can arrange a swift change of venue. We'll march you out of here and continue this interview at the town's police station. Now humour me. What happened?"

"I sat in the adjoining office, working for my father."

"You were fifteen years old. What work could *you* do for the business?"

William's face reddened a touch.

"I put letters into envelopes and stuck stamps on them, ready to take to the Post Office. Dad had me doing clerical work to help. The garage was always busy, and the girl he employed then spent more time chatting on the phone than working. I told him to get rid of her, but Dad said the customers enjoyed seeing a beautiful girl in the office."

"Where was the girl that afternoon? You and your father were alone."

"She finished at three, even in the school holidays. Her mother looked after her daughter."

Luke walked into the adjoining office and sat at the desk.

"Don't mind him," said Gus, "carry on."

"The bell rang, and Dad got up to see to them."

"The front doorbell," asked Gus, "but surely, the door was open?"

"No, back then, we had a pressure strip at the entrance to the forecourt. It warned us when someone drove across it. It was the last thing on Friday afternoon, and Dad said this could be our final deal for the week. He was ever the optimist. Dad got up, went to the front door and stood in the doorway until the customer got out of the car. Then he walked outside to greet him."

"Did he recognise the man?" asked Gus.

"Not as far as I know, but that was Dad's normal way of meeting a customer, whether a regular or someone new. He was always welcoming."

Perhaps you should have watched him more closely, Gus thought.

"What did you see next?" asked Gus.

"I heard the shots—one straight after the other. I ran towards the door. The guy was back in his car, and he floored it as soon as he got it into gear. He almost crashed into the low wall at the exit. He slammed on the brakes and squeezed into the road as he cut someone up. A single-decker bus, I wasn't looking. He drove along London Road like a madman. I tried to help Dad, but there was blood everywhere. I ran back inside and dialled 999. The paramedics arrived in less than five minutes, and the police weren't far behind them. Dad was already dead, I reckon."

In the office next door, Luke shook his head.

He got up and walked back to join Gus.

"When we stood outside earlier, I noticed the plate-glass window," said Luke. "The glass is clear on the side nearest the front door. The left-hand pane contains lots of advertising writing. Because of the pillars and vehicles between these offices and the front windows, you can't see the right-hand pane from that office. You can see the other side, but the advertising obscures the view so much as to make it useless. The only way you could know your father stood in the doorway and waited for the gunman before walking to greet him was to be in this room. If we assume your height at fifteen years of age to have been much as today, then you were standing."

"You can't possibly know that for certain," said William, "you're just guessing."

"Did you expect someone to arrive?" asked Gus. "Was it someone you knew?"

"No, I had no idea who it was," said William, "I told the police that. Alright, I was by this door. I saw Dad walk outside, and I saw the guy raise the gun."

Gus waited for William to continue. Silence reigned.

"It's okay," said Gus, "you were fifteen and scared. So what did you do, duck behind the filing cabinets by the door in case he spotted you?"

William Frayling-Gates nodded.

"So, the description you gave the police was valid," said Gus. "You got a good view of the gunman. Could you remind me of what you saw? One of my colleagues suggests you should close your eyes, blank everything out and tell us what you see in your mind's eye."

William Frayling-Gates did just that. He relaxed for the first time since they arrived.

"The guy was six inches taller than my Dad. He

appeared pale and thin. His hair was cut short, and he'd gelled it, so it stuck up in spikes. He had the hood of his jacket half-on and half off his head. He wasn't trying to hide his face from Dad. I was scared he'd see me, and I was next."

"Can you describe the gun?" asked Gus.

"It was the same as the handguns they use in the movies," said William, "I don't know one from another. He was right-handed; I remember that. I saw the gun come up, and he aimed at Dad's face. I couldn't look anymore."

"You're doing very well," said Gus, "did you hear anyone speak while you were watching or hiding?"

"It happened so fast. Dad moved outside, and when he saw the gun, he asked the guy if it was the money he wanted. The guy didn't answer. He just shot him."

"He never spoke?"

William sat with his eyes closed for several seconds. Then his eyes opened wide.

He'd remembered something.

"The guy shouted one word. The first shot was so loud, and then he fired again straight away. That drowned out whatever he said. I couldn't make it out."

"You're sure you'd never seen him before?" asked Gus. "At the time, you said he was your age."

"I wasn't sure how old he was. It was the police who suggested he was older because of his appearance. They said the pale, skinny look could be because he was a druggie still dressed like a teenager. Now I'm older; I reckon he was five to ten years older than me."

"So, twenty to twenty-five instead of twenty-five to forty?" asked Luke.

"Yeah, no way was he as old as you."

"Well, I'm only twenty-eight," said Luke, "so maybe the gunman was closer to twenty."

"If you say so."

"How was life at home before that day?" asked Gus.

"Fine. Mum and Dad got on great. One of them always took me to football practice. Then the other one collected me afterwards. They both came to Home matches whenever possible."

"What did your Dad tell you about his childhood?" asked Gus.

"He said it was tough. That's why he did so much to keep Mum and me happy."

"Did he mention where he worked before he moved to Marlborough and met your Mum?"

"I don't remember him mentioning anywhere in particular. He worked abroad for a while, but heaven knows what he did. He didn't know about much except cars and football."

"Oh, he played football too, did he? Was he professional?"

"No, he talked of playing for teams in Eastbourne and Hastings in the local leagues. Dad got injured in his early twenties and spent a season doing his Football Association badges so that he could coach or manage someone. He never spoke about whether he completed his badges and ever used them. Dad was only thirty when he moved here. Teams at our level can always use a decent midfielder with experience. If he was injury-free, he had at least five more seasons in him. I suppose my coming along put a stop to that. Dad concentrated on building the business and supporting the team financially. There wasn't enough free time for him to play football."

"Will you be at home later this afternoon?" asked Gus.

"You're seeing Mum at five, aren't you?" asked William. Gus nodded.

"In that case, I'll stop off for a pint at the Roebuck,"

"Just the one, I hope," said Gus.

"Of course," said William, "the season's over, but there's a time and place for everything."

Luke and Gus left William Frayling-Gates in his office and returned to the car park.

As they crossed in front of the showroom, Luke glanced to his left.

"He's on the phone, guv," he said.

"Reporting to Mother, no doubt," said Gus. "Well, we uncovered a few new facts."

"Plus, another angle to follow," said Luke. "The football stories seemed to occupy most of the missing years, so, although William also believed Dennis worked abroad, it couldn't have been for long."

"True," said Gus, "maybe Annie can fill in the missing pieces of that jigsaw."

"We have a couple of hours before she's home, guv. What do you want to do?"

"Find the nearest car park, and then we'll walk through the town centre looking for a decent pub. A soft drink for both of us. If the menu's any good, maybe I'll treat you."

Two hours later, they drove into Shelton Lane. Annie's van stood on the driveway. The door to the double garage was open. There was plenty of space for William's Mercedes to park alongside Annie's Honda HR-V.

"A nice little runabout for the lady of the house," said Luke, "Nicky would love one of those."

"Remember that Annie knows we're coming and possibly has a list of the questions we asked William. Follow my lead."

"Yes, guv," said Luke, hoping he knew where Gus was going.

Annie answered the doorbell on the second ring.

He remembered his first impressions of Maggie Monk, the massage parlour owner. Maggie was smartly dressed and had pride in her appearance, which belied her advancing years. The same applied to Annie Frayling-Gates. Her long, dark curly hair fell over her shoulders, and she could pass for thirty-five, not fifty-five.

Gus realised her electric-blue eyes were challenging him to look away.

"Come through to the sunroom," she said.

Gus let Luke follow her along the hallway. He trailed behind, absorbing every aspect of the rooms he could see. This place reeked of money, or at least someone with too much money and little taste.

Annie sat at the opposite end of the room and waved her guests towards chairs near the back door.

"What did you want to ask me?" said Annie. She took a sip from a tall glass that contained tonic water and a slice of lemon, with added gin or vodka. Unfortunately, there was no offer of refreshments for her visitors.

Gus went through the formalities, and then he waited.

"Why now?" Annie asked, "what's happened to make you interested in looking at the case again?"

"What do you think might have happened?" asked Gus.

"I don't know. Nobody could understand why someone wanted to kill Dennis."

"Did he hit you?"

"Never. How could you say such a thing?"

"You'd be surprised how many murders result from long periods of domestic abuse."

"Well, not in Dennis's case. He was wonderful."

"I understand he suffered a football injury before he met you. Is that correct?"

"Dennis damaged his cruciate ligament, but he made a full recovery. What's that got to do with anything?"

"A person who enjoys a sporting life can turn to outside help when the pain becomes too much to bear."

Luke glanced at Gus.

"Dennis never touched drugs," said Annie. "Look, where are you going with this? The police thought it was someone from a gang who shot him. They asked if he owed money to the wrong people. I told him they weren't referring to the man I knew and loved. That was just fantasy."

"You dismiss the idea that Dennis had a murky past. I find that surprising. What did you know about him before he arrived here in Marlborough? He was thirty years old. That's at least a decade when he could have been up to all sorts. He may have got involved in criminal activities but kept one step ahead of the law. Where did the money come from to finance the garage? He was far from broke when you met him. Was that what attracted you to a man six to nine inches shorter than yourself?"

Annie looked on the verge of tears. Luke wondered whether Gus had gone too far.

He spotted Gus staring out of the window. Muppet. It was his turn to play good cop.

"Where did you meet Dennis for the first time?" he asked.

"At the football club. I'd always been a fan. My Dad took us kids along on Saturday afternoons to give Mum a break. Dennis came to the clubhouse's first social evening of the season in early September of 1991. He'd taken over the garage in London Road and was one of the local businesses that donated the match ball for Home games. Twenty-five pounds worth of advertising provided a good rate of return. We've kept it up after Dennis died."

"You two hit it off straight away?" asked Luke.

"Dennis was charming and knew how to treat a girl. He always dressed smartly, and his accent distinguished him from the local lads. It wasn't love at first sight, but we started seeing one another more often as the months went by."

"You moved in with him two years later, right?"

"Dennis rented a flat in town, close to the business. I stayed there on and off. He never pressured me to make it permanent. It was a poky little place, okay for a bachelor pad but no good for a couple. One weekend he took me around the housing estate near St Mary's school. There was a three-bedroomed semi-detached house for sale. Dennis asked if I'd like to live there. I asked him if that was a proposal. He laughed and said marriage wouldn't change how much he loved me. That was the first time he'd mentioned love. We moved in within a month. I took a long time to get pregnant with William. Nobody's fault, but after he was born in 1995, we both decided enough was enough."

"The showroom continued to be successful," said Luke, "did you get time off for holidays?"

"Not often," sighed Annie, "we spent long weekends on the south coast. Dennis came from Hastings and played football for Eastbourne, Brighton, and Rye teams. They were seaside towns that held memories for him. We travelled over to the Isle of Wight one summer on our own. That was a nice holiday."

"Ventnor?" asked Luke.

"We took the car ferry from Portsmouth to Ryde," said Annie, "then drove to Ventnor. We stayed on a caravan site and toured around the island, stopping at a different spot every day. Do you know Ventnor then?"

"The name cropped up regarding Dennis," said Luke, "did he not mention it?"

"Never," said Annie.

"I asked you earlier how much you knew of his past," said Gus, "his place of birth, for example, where he went to school."

"He came from Hastings and went to school there until he was sixteen."

"Dennis was born in Ventnor in 1961. His teenage mother gave him up for adoption. Dennis spent his early years in care until a childless couple from Hastings adopted him."

"Dennis never said a word about that," said Annie, "he told us he had it tough growing up, and that was why he went the extra mile to make me and William happy."

"You see now why I asked how well you knew your partner? What else did he leave out if he kept his humble beginnings a secret? Where did he work after he left school?"

"Dennis went straight into the garage trade. He was not just selling new or second-hand motors. He knew his way around every type of engine. By the time he bought his first business, Dennis knew the trade inside out."

"When we spoke with William earlier, he was insistent we called him Frayling-Gates. When did you adopt the double-barrelled surname?"

"Several months after Dennis died. I wanted to keep Dennis's name, and mine linked to the business. It helped William retain the goodwill his father built. I employed a manager to bridge Dennis's death and William's old enough to take control. My son worked at weekends and through the holidays learning the tools of the trade."

"William mentioned that Dennis took his FA badges while he recovered from his cruciate ligament injury," said Luke, "did he coach William or any others locally?"

"There was never any call for it," said Annie. "The club already had those things covered when Dennis first arrived. He threw himself into work at the showroom and became a spectator rather than a player or a coach. Once we had William, Dennis played in the garden with him as soon as he could kick a ball, and then at nine years of age, William signed up for the club. Dennis was as proud as punch. He stepped back and let the professionals take over after that."

"It seems a lot of work to study for those badges if he never used them," said Gus.

"Was that a question?" asked Annie.

"No, merely an observation," said Gus, "We've taken up enough of your time for today. We'll get in touch if we have further questions for you or William. Good afternoon."

"I don't know what you expect to get from this review," said Annie accompanying them to the front door. "Not a day passes that I don't think of Dennis and the happy times we shared. Nothing can take those memories from me, but if you find his killer by a miracle, it won't change a damn thing. You can't bring him back."

Gus wasn't sure he could say anything that helped. Sometimes it was least said, soonest mended. He decided this was one of those occasions.

"We'll do our best," said Luke, "it's what the public expects. To try our best for everyone, on every occasion."

Annie Frayling-Gates wasn't listening. She'd already closed the door.

Gus was sitting in the car, waiting as Luke slid into the driver's seat and started the engine.

"Where to, guv?" he asked.

"Home, Luke. Drop me at home, please."

They made the journey back to Urchfont in silence. As Luke turned into the bungalow's driveway, Gus sighed deeply.

"One of those days, guv," said Luke, "we can't win them all."

"She's right, of course, but we still can't rule out a dark secret in those missing years between her saintly Dennis leaving his last garage job and turning up in Newbury at Thornford Motors. The fact he omitted telling her the truth about the first three years of his life is significant. Growing up was tough. That's what Dennis told both Annie and William. There could be three reasons behind that comment. Was his care home experience traumatic? Did the adoptive parents mistreat him? Kids can be cruel. So, was Dennis bullied at school because someone found out he was illegitimate?"

"I thought it interesting that the family spent their holidays near his adoptive parents and even visited his mother's hometown. I wonder if he went looking for her when he was old enough. Despite the money coming into the house, they never holidayed abroad. I wonder if that was significant?"

"Food for thought, Luke," said Gus, "make the most of the weekend. We have plenty of threads to follow next week. Our meetings today have furnished us with far more than I expected."

Gus tapped his colleague on the shoulder and got out of the car. Luke manoeuvred the car in the driveway and soon left for home on the other side of Devizes.

Inside the bungalow, Gus was on the phone.

"Neil, how's Melody?" he asked.

"I brought her home from the hospital an hour ago, guv. She's sleeping now. It's going to take time to recover."

"Whatever it takes, Neil. I'll be in touch early next week. Take care."

One down, three to go, Gus thought. His next call was to Lydia.

"Hi there, guv; how was Marlborough?"

"Productive," Gus replied. "Did you keep busy without me?"

"I was running out of things to do, and DS Mercer got in touch. He had the details of five potential interviewees. I pestered the Hub for a complete breakdown of their criminal record. It will be ready for you first thing on Monday."

"Trefor Davies must have sent those names through to Geoff. I assume that that will be Grenville and Gordon Pearce, plus three more rogues from Marlborough?"

"The very same, guv," said Lydia. "Before you ask, I haven't visited Alex yet. I'm going over there tomorrow afternoon. I'll update you on Monday morning. Was there anything else?"

"No, that covers everything. See you Monday."

Gus wasn't sure how his next call would be received. He needn't have worried. It went to voicemail.

"Hello, Vera, remember me? It's been hectic this week. I've just got home from Marlborough. Luke and I had a meal in one of the High Street pubs mid-afternoon. So I'm just grabbing a sandwich before putting my feet up. Can we get together over the weekend if you've not made other plans? Call me when you're free."

Gus hated leaving messages. He usually dropped into London Road regularly during the week, and he and Vera had ample opportunity to chat and make plans. Gus struggled to recall the last time he'd spoken to her.

His last call was to Suzie Ferris.

"Hey, you," she said, "I've been waiting to speak to you."

"I haven't been home long. Luke dropped me off after a day in Marlborough."

"Oh, I knew you were home," said Suzie, "I tried calling you. Dad said I should leave it until early evening because you were interviewing witnesses. I'm disappointed not to be first on your list of callers. I gave up listening to the engaged tone and decided you could ring me."

Gus laughed.

"I've missed you," he said.

"Good. What are you doing this evening?"

"I'm about to grab a sandwich, get myself a coffee and then run through everything we learned today."

"Boring," sang Suzie, "I'll drive over. You'll be fed and watered by the time I arrive. Then, we can run through everything together while I cuddle up to you."

"As long as you promise not to distract me," said Gus.

"Where's the fun in that?" said Suzie.

Gus realised from the background noise that Suzie was outside in the farmyard and on her way. He gave up the struggle and walked to the kitchen to make a sandwich. He buttered two slices of bread and debated what he fancied.

The phone rang. It was Vera.

"Thanks for calling back," he said.

"I'm shopping for necessities for my new home tomorrow," she said, "how about Sunday? We can have lunch somewhere and take it from there."

"That sounds perfect," said Gus, "leave the restaurant to me this time. We'll take our chances with parking."

"Cheeky. Something is going on at London Road," said

Vera, "the ACC and Geoff Mercer aren't involved. It's higher than that."

"Have any strange men paid you a visit?" asked Gus.

"Not yet, but I get your drift. Yes, the place has got that vibe. As if the you-know-what is due to hit the fan, everyone's holding their breath."

"I don't suppose you've heard any rumours about Ricky Gardiner?"

"That name hasn't been mentioned since you were here on Tuesday. But, as I said, the ACC and Geoff are keeping their heads down. The Chief Constable has stopped ruffling feathers and threatening savage cuts to the backroom staff. She's subdued, to say the least."

Gus heard Suzie's GTI pull up outside. He made a note of another job for the morning. He needed to get the rake out of the garden shed and restore order to the gravel. Suzie tended to accelerate into his driveway and stand on the brakes rather than come to a genteel halt. Stones flew every which way when she arrived.

"I'll let you get on," said Gus, "I think I hear my Domino's pizza delivery outside."

"I'll collect you on Sunday," said Vera, "say, half-past twelve? You can avoid the third-degree from my father that way."

"Whatever you say," said Gus, "goodnight."

"Enjoy your pizza," said Vera.

The doorbell rang just as Vera ended the call. It didn't make Gus feel any better.

"All set?" said Suzie as she breezed through the hallway into the lounge.

"What was that you tried to hide as you rushed past?" asked Gus.

"A cheeky bottle of Merlot from the Margaux region.

My Dad swears by it. Well, he swore when he saw me nick this bottle from the rack. So don't just stand there. Fetch two glasses and a corkscrew."

"I'm not sure you should be drinking alcohol," said Gus. "You're on medication and recovering from a traumatic experience."

"In that case, I shouldn't be driving either," said Suzie, "so it's fortunate that I threw an overnight bag into my car. I didn't risk bringing it indoors in case you thought me brazen."

Gus sighed. He took the bottle into the kitchen, removed the cork, and returned to the lounge with two large glasses.

"Come and sit by me," said Suzie, patting the seat beside her. Gus handed her a glass.

"How was your day?"

"Hold on, young lady," said Gus, "you're the patient. I want to know how you're doing."

"I try not to think about it," said Suzie, "I'd be better at work. If I were busy, I wouldn't have time to think. My parents hover over me like a pregnant mare. Don't panic. You don't have to worry on that score. I mean, that's how mares get when they are foaling. They get anxious and restless."

"John and Jackie love you. It's only natural that they worry."

"This is good, isn't it?"

"What, the wine? Yes, it's excellent."

"No, I meant us, sitting here. You with your arm around me, protecting me. Making me feel wanted."

"We *were* going to run through the new leads we uncovered today," said Gus, "there are a few theories I wish to explore. I asked you to promise not to distract me."

"I won't distract you," said Suzie, finishing her glass of wine. "Hold me and run through your ideas in your head. The best sleep I've had since you rescued me was in the back of the car on our way home. If I lay my head on your chest, I'll be asleep in minutes. Carry me through to the bedroom when you've finished your contemplations."

"Are you sure?" asked Gus.

Suzie kissed his cheek.

"I'm sure," she whispered.

Gus listened to the gentle rhythm of Suzie's breathing and decided he would be asleep in minutes if he didn't think of something else.

He switched his thoughts to Dennis Gates and considered two things.

Why study for qualifications you had no intention of using?

What word had the gunman yelled between the two shots?

Chapter Ten

Monday, 28 May 2018

AS HE WAITED in traffic in the centre of Devizes, Gus wondered what fresh delights lay ahead. The road works were still in evidence. Some of life's elements changed so rapidly that it was hard to cope. Others inched forward. Gus tried to gauge the effect of the worker's efforts since last Monday morning and failed.

The only advantage of these frequent delays was they offered time to reflect.

Suzie Ferris spent the night at the bungalow on Friday. It proved a far more sedate experience than on the previous occasion. Gus still retained a thin streak of rebellion, and he risked her displeasure by finishing the bottle of wine alone. Suzie snored gently beside him while he considered the questions that the day's interviews raised.

It was midnight when Gus carried Suzie into the main bedroom. She stirred slightly, but Gus allowed her to settle again. The overnight bag in the car contained a change of clothing for the morning. There was time enough to fetch it before she woke.

Gus cooked breakfast as Suzie showered alone. They ate together and talked over their plans for the day. Suzie was eager to get home to her horse and her first ride for three weekends. Gus had his list of tasks at the allotment he'd prepared during the week.

"Tomorrow?" asked Suzie as she gathered her things, ready to drive to Worton.

"I've arranged lunch with Vera," Gus said.

"It's difficult, I know," said Suzie, "I'm causing you so much grief."

"I've only got myself to blame."

"It will work itself out."

With that, Suzie kissed him and left. Gus watched her drive through the gateway and remembered the chore he had made a note of yesterday evening. After a brief spell with the rake, he tamed the errant gravel.

Gus strolled along the lane to the allotment and worked until the sun dipped over the horizon. Clemency Benham and Bert Penman pottered about on the adjacent plots for an hour, leaving him to soldier on alone. As they walked towards the Lamb together, Gus thought Bert warned the Reverend that Mr Freeman was pondering more than working. The retired butcher knew he wouldn't welcome the company on days such as today. There was plenty to mull over, both on the case and in his private life.

Gus booked a table at the Waggon & Horses in Harrington End for Sunday lunch when he finally made it home. The extended spell of gardening took it out of him. Gus was in bed and asleep before ten o'clock. Vera arrived at twelve-thirty on the dot the next day. She approved of Gus's choice of restaurant, and after an excellent roast dinner, she drove them to the valley of the stones. The National Trust had cared for the sarsen stones dotted around the Wiltshire countryside for a century. Visitors were familiar with Avebury and Stonehenge, but the land around Piggledene and Lockeridge Dene contained half-buried treasures.

It was a place Gus had never heard of, let alone visited. The sunny Sunday afternoon offered a chance to wander and contemplate the past.

"People have strolled through these meadows to view the ancient rocks for thousands of years," said Vera.

"It's a beautiful spot," Gus agreed, "butterflies and insects can flourish here. They take advantage of the grass-lands. Without the constant roar of traffic on the other side of the hedgerow, it would be idyllic."

As they walked back to her car, Vera stopped.

"You're quieter than normal, Gus," she said, "do you have something on your mind?"

"I've slept with Suzie Ferris," he said.

Vera sighed. "I'm not surprised. Suzie hasn't spoken to me, but it's easy to see she likes you and can be very persuasive."

"I feel such a heel, Vera. When we met, we were both looking for something more than companionship. We got on so well together that I kept asking myself what was wrong with me. I felt content but not wretched like I did when I fell in love with Tess all those years ago. Now, I doubt whether I could care as deeply about anyone as I did for Tess. If I did, then I would have spurned Suzie's advances. The unex-pected attention flattered me, and I selfishly took advantage."

"I understand," said Vera. "We're good together, and neither of us ever looked to take things further. We both value our independence. I'll have my new home in a week or two. You have the bungalow where your memories of Tess surround you. I never had designs on moving things to a different level. I hoped we would see one another regularly and continue enjoying our relationship's physical side. Perhaps we were both selfish."

"Where do we go from here?" Gus asked.

"Back to my place," said Vera, slipping her arm through Gus's as they walked back across the meadow to her car. "You'll decide which way you want to go when ready. Suzie might move on. She might dig her heels in and stay. Who knows? I'm going nowhere. We'll always remain friends, no matter what. Come on, let's make the most of the rest of the day."

Gus heard a car horn nearby. It sounded urgent. He realised the lights had changed, and the traffic was moving again. As he motored towards the Old Police Station, he tried to understand how the female mind worked. Gus shook his head. He could never hope to fathom that on a short journey of ten miles. Even when roadworks made him fifteen minutes late.

Luke and Lydia had swapped their weekend stories upstairs in the Crime Review Team office.

Luke and Nicky attended a raucous party on Saturday night. Sunday was a day of rest.

Lydia spent the weekend with Alex and brought good news and bad news.

"Many people who abuse oxycodone start taking a prescribed amount," she told Luke. "As their body develops a tolerance to the drug, they need a higher dose to maintain the same relief. The transition from use to abuse to addiction can be a quick process. Oxycodone is a powerful drug and offers welcome relief to people suffering from the pain Alex has had to bear. It's hard to stay in control. His doctor prescribed it for the moderate-to-severe pain he suffered after coming out of the hospital to continue his recovery. He tried to do too much too soon. Alex rushed to quit using the wheelchair, and it was painful to watch him forcing himself to use the crutches. He was desperate to dispense with those too. All he ever wanted was to get back on that motorbike of his. Even if the pursuit rider role was in the past, he still wanted to recapture his love of the open road."

"What symptoms did you first notice that made you suspect he took more than was good for him?" asked Luke.

"His reaction to day-to-day events seemed off," said Lydia. "When I felt sad, he felt happy. Alex was always confident and relaxed, no matter what the situation. Nothing stressed him. In the afternoons, I noticed he got sleepy. He never suffered drowsiness in the office, but then suddenly, he did."

Both Luke and Lydia heard the lift. Gus Freeman was in the building.

"How long will it be before he's back?" asked Luke.

"That's what I want to hear," said Gus, "is this my Monday update on Alex?"

"Yes, guv," said Lydia, "he's accepted that he's got a problem. So now we have to wean him off the oxycodone and reassess the methods he uses to regain full fitness, or as close to it as possible."

"Alex is lucky to have you there to help him, Lydia," said Gus.

"What's the schedule for the week, guv?" asked Luke.

"It's your turn in the office today, Luke," said Gus,

"Lydia and I are off to the Isle of Wight later. Do we have a name for Dennis Gates's birth mother?"

Luke checked the original murder file. He shook his head.

"Nothing listed, guv. I'll call William and ask when his father celebrated his birthday. There can't have been too many births in Ventnor in 1961. We can narrow the search further by ignoring boys where the father's name appears on the records. Give me an hour."

"Lydia, get us booked on a ferry crossing. I prefer Portsmouth to Ryde, but Lymington to Yarmouth will do the trick."

"On it, guv," said Lydia, "did you hear from Neil?"

"Melody came home on Friday evening," said Gus, "I told Neil to take as long as he needs. I don't expect to see him in this office before next Monday at the earliest."

Gus updated the Freeman Files with his notes on Friday's interviews. Meanwhile, Luke and Lydia beavered away on the tasks he'd set them. At ten o'clock, Gus needed a coffee.

"As you're busy, I'll become reacquainted with the Gaggia. Three coffees are coming up."

Fifteen minutes later, Luke and Lydia were ready to report their findings.

"It wasn't hard tracing the lady in question, guv," said Luke. "There was one surprise, though. Perhaps I was naïve. I thought Gates would be the surname of the adoptive parents."

"Interesting," said Gus, "continue."

"Christine Gates gave birth to a baby boy on the tenth of June 1961 in Ventnor. Christine registered her baby's name as Dennis. He weighed in at seven pounds fourteen ounces."

"Somewhere in that murder file, there must be details of the adoptive parents," said Gus, "while he lived under their roof, surely he carried their name? Did Trefor Davies and his team check the school records to see they had the right chap? It may be quicker to ask the mother. OK, when do we leave, Lydia?"

"The ferries run every hour on the hour from Lymington, guv. A forty-minute crossing to Yarmouth and a thirty-minute drive will get us to Ventnor. I booked us on the one o'clock ferry."

Gus checked his watch. The old Ford Focus would enjoy a day out. The furthest they'd driven in ages was to and from work.

"Let's get going then," he said, "we must grab a pasty or something to keep body and soul together."

"That's Cornwall, guv," said Lydia, "I'm not sure the Isle of Wight is famous for any culinary delights."

After a calm crossing, Gus drove them along the west coast road from Yarmouth and across the south coast to Ventnor.

"What a beautiful place to live, guv," said Lydia.

"The place will crawl with holidaymakers in a few weeks. It's already busy. That road we just came along must be bleak in winter. I wouldn't fancy it. Life's always about balance, Lydia, you know that."

Christine Gates answered the door of her two-up, two-down cottage eighty yards behind The Esplanade. The seventy-three-year-old woman was short and stocky. She peered up at Gus and Lydia through thick glasses.

"I don't buy at the door," she said, "can't you read the sign?"

"Christine Gates?" asked Gus, "we'd appreciate a word,

madam. My name is Freeman, and I am a consultant with Wiltshire Police. My colleague is Ms Logan Barre. We're here to ask you about your son, Dennis."

"You had better come indoors. I don't know how to tell you this, but Dennis is dead."

"We know that, Christine," said Lydia, "can I call you Christine? I'm Lydia."

They followed the little old lady into a tiny front room. Everything was neat and tidy. Gus thought he could sit in the middle of the room and almost touch the four walls.

"We know you gave birth to Dennis in June 1961," said Lydia, "had you decided to give him up for adoption early in the pregnancy?"

"I didn't even realise I was expecting," said Christine, "I was still at school. I'd gone with several boys, and I was never sure which was the father. Nobody came forward to accept responsibility. They were different times on the island back then. I was fortunate not to get sent to the mental asylum. That's where unmarried mothers went, you know."

"I read about that," said Lydia, "it sounds barbaric now, but as you say, different times."

"As soon as I had Dennis, they let me hold him for a while. I gave him the name I'd chosen, and then they took him away. I didn't see him again until he came to find me."

"A family from Hastings adopted Dennis, didn't they?" asked Gus.

"That's right. When Dennis first came to see me, I wished I'd kept the little chap no matter what my parents thought. My heart went out to him. He wouldn't have suffered as much as he did."

"Dennis went into care for three years, I believe," said Gus.

"Dennis was happy while he was there, he said. It was Mr Giles that was so cruel to him."

"Giles?" asked Gus, "so when they adopted him, he became Dennis Giles?"

"Dennis was my name for him. His new mother chose to call him Danny, after Danny Williams, the chap who sang Moon River. When my son came to look me up, he was called Danny Giles."

"When was that, Christine?" asked Lydia.

"Dennis was twenty-one," she replied, "just back from a three-month working holiday in Menorca. He had a lovely tan. I think he went there to get away from home. I asked him about his childhood. Dennis said the days at the home were the happiest days of his life. When he moved to Hastings, his so-called father abused him physically and mentally. Dennis said he was lucky if he only got struck with the back of his father's hand. When his father was in a foul mood, he'd take his belt to him. I asked how his mother reacted. Dennis said his mother knew better than to open her mouth. His father was a cruel and unforgiving man."

"When did Dennis leave home?" asked Gus.

"When he was twenty," said Christine, "Dennis wanted to leave earlier. But, once he could fight back, his father left him alone and concentrated his attention on his wife. So Dennis stayed to protect her."

"What prompted the move to Menorca?" asked Gus, "we understood Dennis played football for various teams in the county and worked in local garages."

"Dennis loved his football and working on cars," said Christine. "It was in the autumn when he came to find me. Dennis told me he'd try his hand at something different and applied to be a holiday rep. My son stuck with it for three months and then decided it wasn't for him. Dennis returned to find his mother on her own. His father had died six weeks earlier from a heart attack. They were free of him at last. Dennis offered to stay with her, but she convinced him to make his own life."

"So, Dennis returned to working garages and playing football until he got injured," said Gus, "I don't suppose you know what happened next?"

"Dennis visited me several times, Mr Freeman, after that first time. He came to the island on crutches once to tell me he'd done serious damage to his ligament and couldn't play. Dennis told me he was learning to be a coach. The club wanted an assistant coach for their Under-16 side. That's when it went wrong for him."

"This would be in 1983 or thereabouts," said Gus, "why did things go wrong?"

Christine Gates stared at her lap.

"The team Dennis trained was a girls' team. He was twenty-two, and although he went out with girls, I could tell he was shy and vulnerable. I blame that on his father. Dennis was young for his age, Mr Freeman. The next summer, Dennis and his girlfriend came to Ventnor and stayed at the caravan park. Her name was Gemma. Dennis was so proud of her when he brought her to meet me. The next thing I heard was the police arrived from Lewes to arrest him. Gemma was only fifteen, and her parents thought she was staying with a school friend. The young lovers ran away, thinking they could stay here forever. Dennis never forced himself on her, Mr Freeman. Gemma loved him, and he loved her, but the law's the law. He was on remand for months. Dennis got sent to prison for five years. He served three years and came out in 1988."

"While he was in prison, his adoptive mother died and left everything to him," said Lydia,

Christine Gates nodded.

"He always loved her. Dennis didn't want to let her down. That's why he kept the name Danny Giles until he came out of prison and resumed his life again."

No wonder they could never find a police record for Dennis Gates, thought Gus. The inheritance started him in business at Thornford Motors in Newbury, and then three years later, he moved to Marlborough. Things began to gel now.

"Did you continue to see Dennis?" asked Lydia.

"Oh, yes," said Christine, her smile lit up her face. "He brought Annie for a holiday; then one summer, they arrived with William, my grandson."

That was odd, thought Gus. Annie Frayling-Gates mentioned the Isle of Wight holiday but nothing about meeting Dennis's birth mother.

"How did you meet?" he asked.

"They stayed at the same caravan park where Dennis brought Gemma," said Christine, "I was still working back then. Dennis knew where I'd be during the daytime. I understood why he didn't introduce me. He never told Annie about his past. Who can blame him? So, it was our secret. I worked in a cafe on the seafront where we served the best cream teas in town. Dennis brought Annie in every afternoon that week. We chatted when he came to the counter to pay. It was enough for me to see how happy they were. At last, he was living the life I wished for him. I was over the moon when they brought William with them a couple of years later. I couldn't resist touching his chubby cheek as he sat in his buggy. Annie thought I was just friendly. She recognised me as the lady who served their cream teas on the last occasion they holidayed on the island. She never suspected a thing. One evening, Annie sent

Dennis for a takeaway and cans of lager. He called in to see me on his way back to the caravan. He was so happy. Everything was going well with the business, family life was terrific, and he'd found me again."

"Did they return to Ventnor again?" asked Lydia.

"No," said Christine, "Dennis sent flowers on my birthday every year. He posted cards at Christmas, including letters and photos that kept me in touch with how William was getting on. Dennis was so busy. It was difficult to get away, and there was always the risk the past would come back to hurt him. He paid for his so-called crime; he deserved his happiness."

"How did you learn of his death?" asked Lydia.

"We do get the newspapers over here, believe it or not. It was a shock, I can tell you. I never believed that rubbish that Dennis got involved with criminals. That wasn't my son. He was as honest as the day is long."

"Did the police ever get in touch?" asked Gus.

"I never heard a word from the police," said Christine, "I sat and waited for a knock at the door, but it never came. When I thought about it, I realised they wouldn't have known to look for me, would they? I gave him up at birth, so the police would have thought that was it. They didn't know Dennis came looking for me, and we'd kept in contact for thirty years. You don't have to inform anyone officially, do you? When the police discovered that both Giles were dead, they dreamed up this underworld connection and stopped looking for answers from his past. Dennis's secret died with him, thank goodness. I wouldn't want Annie and William to have their memories of him tainted."

Gus felt this was becoming déjà vu all over again.

"You've been very helpful, Miss Gates," he said, "we'll let you get on with your day. If we have any further questions, we'll call you. Could you give your number to my colleague, please?"

"Of course," said Christine.

Gus was already out of the door and walking to the car. Lydia scribbled the phone number in her notebook and chased after him.

"Are we in a rush to get the next ferry, guv?" she asked.

"Not really," he replied, "we can catch another one. I'll get you home to Chippenham before ten o'clock. All things being equal."

"What did you make of that conversation then, guv?"

"Christine Gates filled gaps in our knowledge, and then she raised further questions. Questions to which we don't have the answers. Let's drive to Yarmouth and discuss the case en route."

The late afternoon sun made the journey back to the north of the island a pleasant one. Gus considered what they had learned and then spoke.

"We can explain the reason now for the gaps in the timeline DI Trefor Davies didn't fill in the original investigation. As Christine said, why ask a woman who hasn't seen her child for forty-nine years about his previous life? The natural source of information was the adoptive parents in Hastings. Davies and his team checked that place first and found that both parents died before Gates even arrived in Marlborough."

"The thing that puzzled me was the name," said Lydia. "Christine didn't want to keep her son, but she took the trouble to name him Dennis. He kept that throughout the three years he spent in care. When he got adopted, he had to get used to being called Danny. Could it be as simple as Giles and Gates being similar? A lazy detective missed the difference. After all, the first name initial was the same."

"Youngsters shorten names all the time," said Gus, "Dennis could become Den or Denny in the playground. The detectives might confuse it with Danny, but it shouldn't have happened."

"It was Danny Giles who got sent to prison for having sex with a minor," said Lydia, "his name wouldn't appear on the sex offender's registry, would it?"

"That offence occurred in the early Eighties," said Gus. "The register started in 1997. The courts were still operating under an Act for Dennis's case from the mid-Fifties, and changes were long overdue. There are more than enough names on that registry without adding names of people from previous decades."

"We got *some* answers, guv," said Lydia, "what's left to discover?"

"No matter who we talk to, the underworld angle looks to be a non-starter. The young girl, Gemma that Dennis ran away with is now in her early fifties. We must find her and interview her. Despite what Christine Gates said, we still need to find her son's killer."

"Is Gemma our only hope, guv?" asked Lydia as they entered Yarmouth.

"I can't see any other potential leads, can you?" said Gus. "If you want to unpick the statements of everyone who knew Dennis Gates while he lived in Marlborough, go ahead. Everyone thought him a saint. William swears blind he didn't recognise the killer. We're looking for a stranger who wanted Dennis dead. A stranger who shouted something with venom at Dennis between each shot."

Gus and Lydia took a break from discussing the case as the ferry threaded its way across the channel to Lymington. The scenery was breathtaking. While waiting for the cars ahead to drive ashore, Gus realised he was hungry.

"Do you want to get something to eat here?" he asked.

"A pasty?" asked Lydia.

"I think we can better that. Lymington's got a few places with a great reputation. The Italian restaurant near the harbour's the closest. Is that OK?"

"Bella, guv," said Lydia.

Chapter Eleven

Tuesday, 29 May 2018

"HELLO, SAILOR," said Luke as Lydia arrived in the CRT office, "how was the Isle of Wight?"

"Beautiful," said Lydia, "we were lucky to have a calm crossing in both directions. Gus treated me to an Italian meal on our way home. All very civilised."

"Did you squeeze in any work while you were there?" asked Luke.

"Christine Gates was lovely. I felt sorry for her. Christine never married. One mistake when just a child altered her life forever. Crazy, isn't it? Dennis searched her out after an unhappy childhood. They formed a bond, and then she met Annie and William. They were never aware of who she was. I want to ring Annie and put her in touch with Christine, but that could be so wrong."

"You have been busy," said Luke, "but how does any of that help us?"

"There was another person we learned about yesterday, a young girl called Gemma who played football for a girls' team. Dennis fell in love with her, and they had sex when she was fifteen. They ran away to Ventnor, and Gemma met Dennis's mother. Gemma's parents called the police, and Dennis got arrested on the Isle of Wight. He was taken back to East Sussex and later jailed for five years. Dennis came out after three years to learn his adoptive mother died, leaving him everything in her will."

"That's how Dennis financed the garage in Newbury that started him on the road to Marlborough. Where's Gus? I'd better search for this girl, Gemma. Let's start with court cases in Lewes in 1985. Her name might not be there because she was a minor."

"That's Gus now," said Lydia, "if you can't find her in 1985, then dig into births in the Rye area in 1967."

Gus Freeman came through the lift doors at pace. He looked like a man on a mission.

"Right," he began, "we need details of a young woman born in 1967."

"On it, guv," said Luke, "Lydia set the ball rolling. I'll have everything that ties in with the court case and her history within the hour. That should allow you two to update the Freeman Files with everything you gleaned yesterday."

"Terrific," said Gus, "We'll switch places today. Luke, you can go with Lydia. I'll dig into the backgrounds of the tearaways that DI Davies forwarded. Trefor promised to send details of extra lads from the Swindon area too. Any sign of those, Luke?"

"No guv."

"I'll badger Trefor Davies again as soon as I've updated these files. Okay, heads down. We're nearly there."

Luke and Lydia shared a glance. Here we go again. Gus has a clue, and he's not sharing it with us. Forty-five minutes later, Gus was itching to get his team out of the door. Time was pressing.

"What have you turned up, Luke?" asked Gus.

"Gemma Mailey, fifty-one years old. She married Dave in 1987. He's a bricklayer—three children; Zack, twenty-nine, Jack, twenty-seven, and Zoe, twenty-five. The parents live in Folkestone. The kids have left home but live in the neighbourhood."

"What was Gemma's maiden name?" asked Gus.

"Tatum, guv," said Luke.

"Any siblings?"

"A younger brother, Nathan, forty-seven now. I haven't traced his whereabouts yet."

"I'll keep digging. You and Lydia crack on with making it to Folkestone. Do you have contact details for the family members?"

Luke walked across to Gus's desk and handed him a slip of paper.

"That's it. Off you go. I'll warn the Mailey family some-one's on their way. They'll be available for an interview. I can be very persuasive when the need arises."

Luke and Lydia were in the lift and heading for the car park in seconds.

"The pace has suddenly picked up, hasn't it?" said Lydia.

"Gus knows something we don't, as usual," said Luke.

"You hope," scoffed Lydia, "he didn't even tell you what to ask them. Any ideas?"

"Plenty of time," said Luke, "it's a three-hour drive via the M3 and Maidstone. I'll think of something."

In the CRT office, Gus Freeman was hunting for Nathan Tatum.

In Folkestone, Dave and Gemma Mailey lived on Coniston Road. The detached property looked well-maintained from the kerbside, which Luke thought odd for a bricklayer. But, where he came from, tradespeople were notorious for doing everyone else's maintenance jobs, and the urgency to tackle their own was negligible.

"I wonder if it's as good on the inside?" he asked Lydia.

"I'm more concerned about what welcome we'll get," she replied.

A middle-aged woman with bleached-blonde hair answered the door at number 375. The housecoat looked too small, and it was hard to imagine sport playing a role in her current life. So, this was Gemma Tatum, thought Lydia. The intervening thirty-five years since she ran away with Danny Giles had not been kind.

"You must be the coppers I'm expecting," she said.

"I'm DS Luke Sherman from Wiltshire Police. My colleague is Lydia Logan Barre. Our boss called you earlier. I hope your husband, Dave, is with you?"

"Dave's here," said Gemma, "but he's not happy losing money hanging around for the likes of you."

Lydia felt uncomfortable. Gemma Mailey directed that comment at her.

"We just want an informal chat at this stage," said Luke, sensing the need to lead the conversation. "Why don't we run through what we need from you today?"

"Sit in the lounge. I'll call Dave in from the garden. He's having a fag."

"Let's chat alone first," said Luke, "you'll understand why in a minute."

Gemma led the way into the lounge. Luke indicated to

Lydia that she should stand by the door. He didn't want Dave Mailey to come in just yet.

"We're from a Crime Review Team set up by Wiltshire Police to look into unsolved cases," said Luke. "Eight years ago, a murder took place in Marlborough. The owner of a successful garage died in front of his fifteen-year-old son. The victim was Dennis Gates, forty-nine. Does that name ring any bells?"

Gemma shook her head.

Lydia wondered whether the blank look was genuine or something she'd perfected after years of practice. But then, she spotted Dave Mailey watching her from the kitchen. He quickly entered the hallway.

"You might know him better as Danny Giles," said Luke.

Gemma gasped, and her hand flew to her mouth.

"God no, not Danny! I never knew."

Dave Mailey brushed Lydia aside and lumbered through the lounge door.

"Who's Danny Giles? What's this about, anyway?" he demanded.

Luke wished he would sit down. Dave Mailey was a giant of a man with hands like dinner plates.

"Sit down, Dave," snapped Gemma, "you never met him. He was part of my life way before we met."

"After you and Danny returned from the Isle of Wight, did you see him again?" asked Luke. He kept a weather eye on Dave Mailey. The guy was seething. The Best Actor Oscar was a certainty if this was a performance.

"I didn't have to go to court," said Gemma, "Danny pleaded guilty. My parents never let me out of their sight for ages. Dave came to the house to work and got on with my Dad. We started seeing one another, and that was that."

"What did this guy do to you?" asked Dave.

"Nothing I didn't want him to do," snapped Gemma, "get over yourself. I loved Danny. If I'd been sixteen instead of fifteen years and five months, you wouldn't have had a look-in."

"We just need one more thing from you, Mr Mailey," said Luke, "and then we'll be on our way. Can you confirm your whereabouts on Friday, the twentieth of August 2010, between two o'clock and five?"

"Not off the top of my head. I can check my accounts to see where I worked that week."

"Where the actual property was won't matter," sneered Gemma Mailey. "You always finish early on Friday. They'll need to check with the landlord of the closest pub."

"The guy on the phone wanted us to have the kids on standby," said Dave ignoring his wife. "They're at work. Do we need to call them and get them over here?"

"That won't be necessary, Mr Mailey," said Luke, "just ring this number with the details of where you were on that date. We'll follow it up. If everything tracks, as I believe it will, we won't need to bother you again. We're sorry to have brought you such sad news, Mrs Mailey. I know it was a long time ago, but first loves can be memorable, can't they?"

Gemma walked with them to the front door.

"You said he lived in Marlborough? Why did he change his name?" she asked.

"I suppose he wanted the past to stay in the past," said Lydia.

Gemma Mailey stared at Lydia and looked over her shoulder. Her husband, Dave, still sat in the chair in the lounge.

"Yeah, well, it won't now, will it, thanks to you."

Gemma Mailey slammed the door.

"Ouch," said Luke, "maybe Gus could have handled that better."

"You did the right thing separating them at the outset," said Lydia, "but there was no stopping him when Dave came in from the garden, sorry."

"Don't apologise. Gemma and Dave had nothing to do with it, did they? I wonder if Gus knew that all along?"

"I'll call him," said Lydia, "to update him on what little we learned. Perhaps he's traced Nathan Tatum by now. In which case, we can look him up this afternoon before driving back."

"That sounds like a plan," said Luke.

Lydia made the call.

"Hi, Gus. We're done with Dave and Gemma Mailey. A charming couple, she's a closet racist, and he's not someone you'd wish to bump into in a dark alley late at night. Luke and I don't believe they knew anything about the murder. Dave Mailey will provide an alibi in due course. Can we visit Nathan Tatum while we're in the area?"

"Nathan Tatum won't be going anywhere. He's in HMP Lewes, the same Category B prison that housed Danny Giles all those years ago."

"Will we need to book an appointment, guv?" said Lydia, "or can we drop by and ask to see him for an hour?"

"I'll get DS Mercer to arrange something," said Gus, "forget it for today. Come back to the office."

"Did you catch any of that?"

"Gus needs us back in the office. Which, translated, probably means Nathan Tatum isn't our man."

Luke began the long trek to Wiltshire. They'd travelled a fair old distance for little reward.

"Blow this," he said, "why don't we stop in Maidstone for a snack before we go back?"

"I could get used to this," said Lydia, "Gus wined and dined me last night. Alex will get jealous."

"Alex has nothing to worry about," said Luke, "and we're not drinking."

"Your partner, Nicky, is a Nicholas, isn't he," said Lydia.

"He is; we've been together for six years. We don't hide it, but I don't advertise it at work. Things are better than they were, but people like me and Sandra Plunkett still have a long way to go before every scrap of prejudice disappears."

Luke spotted a coffee house with a Conan Doyle connection that seemed the right spot for two detectives to take afternoon tea. It fitted the bill perfectly, and by four o'clock, they were back on the M20. It was close to six o'clock when they reached the CRT office.

They should have guessed. Gus was still there.

"Call off the search party," he called, to nobody in particular, "the wanderers have returned."

"The motorways were a nightmare, guv. Are we driving to Lewes tomorrow?" asked Luke.

"Unless Nathan Tatum escapes overnight, he'll be waiting for you and me to arrive."

"What have you planned for me, guv?" asked Lydia.

"I want both of you to get home straight away and be back first thing bright-eyed. You can then update the Freeman Files, and after that, Luke and I will leave. Your task, Lydia, is to see whether any of the names I've worked on served a sentence somewhere that overlapped with Nathan Tatum. This current spell in Lewes is not his first rodeo. At sixteen, he started at the Youth Offenders Institute at Cookham Wood, next door to HMP Rochester. Since then, he's been a frequent flyer."

"With a propensity to violence?" asked Luke.

"I wouldn't class him as a stone-cold killer, no," said Gus, "that's why tomorrow could be enlightening."

Luke and Lydia said their farewells and made for the lift. Gus checked through his list of questions for the following day, and five minutes later, he was on his way home.

Wednesday, 30 May 2018

GUS GAZED out of his kitchen window at the threatening clouds. There were rain showers overnight, and those leaden skies promised more later. These were not the driving conditions he preferred for a trip across the country. Maybe he should have told Luke to collect him on his way through. Too late now; he'd suggested they work at the Old Police Station for a while before heading for Lewes.

When Gus reached home yesterday evening, he hadn't felt up to more gardening. He sat at home with a light meal and a glass of wine, trying to make sense of the interviews they'd completed so far. He strove to plot a route through the maze and unmask the killer. The motivation was the stumbling block.

Nathan Tatum might have felt aggrieved when his sister's boyfriend ran away with her, but he was barely out of short trousers at the time of the court case. Gemma was unaware that Danny Giles was dead, mainly because she didn't know he'd changed his name to Dennis Gates. How on earth could she or Nathan know who to search for if they sought retribution? Why wait thirty-five years if the need for revenge was that desperate?

Gus thought of the names Trefor Davies gave him.

Any of the five Marlborough lads were capable of violence, but the method of Dennis Gates's murder was a step change to the thuggery that stamped their criminal records. Gus racked his brains, trying to find a motive to justify one of those five lads killing such a popular figure.

William didn't recognise the gunman. He was sure his father didn't know him. That's when the lightbulb moment occurred.

This morning as he drove towards Devizes and onwards to the Old Police Station, he thought he could see a glimmer of light. Today's meetings were crucial.

Gus was surprised to find Luke and Lydia hard at work. They must have thought 'first thing' meant the early starts they made last week when searching for Suzie Ferris. But, no matter, they could take it more carefully driving to Lewes now.

"How are we fixed?" he asked.

"I'm ready to leave in five minutes, guv," said Luke, "do you need me to drive?"

"You had a full day of it yesterday, Luke. I'll do my share; don't nag at me if we potter along at forty miles per hour."

"I've finished updating the files, guv," said Lydia, "is there anyone on this list I should concentrate on, or shall I just run through the lot in alphabetical order?"

"You think I've worked out the killer's identity," said Gus, "but that's not the case. Take pot luck if you wish. Just don't leave any stone unturned. Our interview with Nathan Tatum starts at twelve-thirty. I expect to be back here before five, but I don't mind if you slope off before we return, as you started early. Are you bringing Alex with you tomorrow?"

"He asked whether you minded him attending Terry Davis's funeral, guv."

"Of course, I don't mind," said Gus, "he's still a team member."

Gus indicated to Luke that he was ready to leave. They headed for the lift.

Gus turned and called Lydia.

"When you get a match, call me at once."

"Got it, guv."

Lydia called Alex with the news as soon as the lift doors closed.

"Not quite the same trip as yesterday, Luke," said Gus, "nice to have variety, isn't it?"

"Yes, guv. We had the best of the weather, too, by the looks of it."

HMP Lewes looked as wet and miserable as Gus felt three hours later as they negotiated the secure entrance. Once inside the building, they followed their escort to an interview room. At twelve-thirty on the dot, two prison officers marched Nathan Tatum into the room and sat him facing them. The prison officers took two steps back and stood on either side of Tatum. Luke wondered whether they expected trouble.

Gus glanced at the habitual criminal sat opposite him. He remembered the lyrics to the old Bo Diddley track. You can't tell a book by looking at its cover. But, somehow, Nathan Tatum gave the lie to that. His shaven head, tattoos and overall aura of menace left the man little choice of occupation.

"Thank you for agreeing to this meeting, Nathan," said Gus, "no doubt you're glad of a few extra minutes out of your cell. My name is Freeman, and I am a consultant with Wiltshire Police. My colleague is DS Sherman. Our Crime

Review Team is taking a fresh look into the murder of Dennis Gates in August 2010."

"Never heard of him," said Tatum.

"We know you didn't do it, Nathan," said Gus, "you were in Whitemoor, Cambridgeshire. You do love to see different parts of the country, don't you?"

"Will this take much longer? I could be counting raindrops."

"Let me tell you a story, Nathan," said Gus. "When you were a young lad, yet to become familiar with the inside of a cell, your sister, Gemma, fell in love with a man called Danny Giles."

"That guy was a pervert. He made the most of an injury to wangle himself a part-time job training underage girls to kick a football. Waste of bleeding time. What do women know about sports? How many girls did he have his way with before he snared our Gemma? Eh, answer me that. No, you can't because nobody bothered to ask. Gemma went all gooey on him and jumped in his car when he said, let's go to the Isle of Wight. Pure as the driven snow she was until he got his filthy hands on her."

"You were eleven years old at the time?"

"I don't know what that has to do with anything. My old man was climbing the walls. He would have killed the scrote if he'd caught hold of him. But, instead, he laid into me every day they were missing, telling me never to forget what's right and wrong."

"He wasted his breath, didn't he, Nathan? You were in Cookham Wood before you turned sixteen. You've shown a complete disregard for what's right and what's wrong ever since."

"I can't deny I've done bad things," said Nathan, "but I was never a child molester."

"It's time to move on to the rest of the story, Nathan," said Gus, checking his mobile for a text message from Lydia. There was nothing.

"Danny Giles came here to HMP Lewes in 1985 to serve a five-year sentence. He left after three years in 1988."

"Typical," said Nathan, "the nonces get preferential treatment because they spend their time hiding from real men. But, then, the warden falls for the bullshit that they're model prisoners or seen the error of their ways. Where's the justice in that?"

"I'd get through this much quicker if you stopped interrupting," said Gus, "any idea where you were towards the end of the last century?"

"Dorchester?" replied Nathan.

"Correct," said Gus.

"I want to return to my cell now," said Nathan, "you're just fishing."

Gus felt a vibration in his jacket pocket. Well done, Lydia, saved by the bell.

He read the text message and passed the phone to Luke.

"Could you make a note of that, please, DS Sherman?"

"Certainly, guv," said Luke.

"Yes, Nathan, you were in HMP Dorchester. One point for that correct answer. For two points, who was your cellmate?"

"A bloke from up Swindon way. It was a long time ago."

"The name was Grant Pearce, who came from Marlborough. Remember him? Someone with a string of offences longer than your arm. He was born in 1959 and had already spent several years in prison. You were in your mid-twenties and came to Dorchester with a reputation. Most inmates feared you. Pearce didn't, and you listened to what he had to say because he never took a backwards step."

"It's what gets you through your first stretch," said Nathan, "the old lags show you the ropes. After that, you listen and survive, or ignore them and get knifed in the showers. If you're lucky."

"I'm going to be creative now, Nathan. You can correct me if I go wildly off course. Grant asked after your family. He told you about his sons, Gordon and Grenville, who were eleven and nine years old. I don't know if you've kept in touch. They're following in their father's footsteps."

"I've never met either of them. That's the truth."

"Did you have the odd family photo with you in Lewes?"

"No comment."

"I reckon Grant had photos of his boys, possibly the attack dog too. Her name is Moira, his wife. She's in Eastwood Park. Moira had a falling out with three other ladies on a bingo night eighteen months ago over how to share a jackpot. It took the staff ages to clear the broken glass from the velour seats in the hall. At the A&E, the nurses stopped counting stitches when it reached three figures. You carried a photo of your parents and your sister, didn't you?"

"What if I did?"

"On a quiet night in your cell, you told Grant Pearce about Danny Giles and Gemma. He said much the same thing as your Dad. Along the lines that wrongs need to get put right. Where did the photo come from?"

"What photo?"

"A photo that included Danny Giles. Give me credit. I've done this before."

Nathan Tatum shifted in his chair.

"Gemma sent it to me. I asked my mother to get Gemma to send me a football team photo. He was on it."

"What did Grant Pearce say?"

"I can't remember."

"Pearce took a long hard look at it and told you he'd been here in this same prison between 1985 and 1988. He recognised Danny Giles. He thought three years wasn't nearly enough. What did the two of you agree on then, Nathan?"

"No comment."

"Come along. I can't do all the work. Well, I'm not really, because a colleague in the Crime Review Team provided me with most of the story links. I'm filling in the gaps. The assistant coach wouldn't be prominent in a team photo, so Danny was at one end. You cut it off and gave it to Grant Pearce."

"As I said, you're fishing. You do whatever it takes to survive a sentence. There are people here who would pay good money for a photo of a young man to get them through the cold winter nights. It was a long time ago. Maybe I swapped it for tobacco."

"Did Gemma ever ask why you needed that photo?"

"Not that I remember. I was surprised Gemma kept anything to remind her of him. Gemma married Dave a couple of years after Giles went to prison. She also sent me a photo of them and their three kids while I was in Dorchester, so what?"

"I spoke with the man's birth mother," said Gus, "she never doubted that Gemma and her son were in love. That's who they visited on the Isle of Wight, you know. Danny Giles ran away with your sister to stay near his real mother."

"Very touching," snarled Nathan Tatum, "it doesn't change a thing."

"It must have irked you and Grant Pearce that no

matter who you asked or where you looked, you never found Danny Giles."

"You're the only one who thinks we did."

"If you had known he was adopted and realised his birth mother could be alive somewhere, Danny Giles could have died earlier."

"Are you telling me he's dead? Well, put the flags out."

"Never play poker, Nathan. When we began this trip down memory lane, I told you the reason for this visit. We were investigating the murder of Dennis Gates in August 2010. You shrugged and said you'd never heard of him. I've been doing this job a long time, Nathan; I noticed the slight twitch below your left eye. It made another fleeting appearance when you pretended not to recall the photo. Christine Gates told us that after his adoptive parents died, her son switched to the name she gave him at birth. So you needed to hunt for Dennis Gates, not Danny Giles."

"I was in Whitemoor when he died, if you've forgotten, and I never knew anyone called Dennis Gates."

"We'll let these officers return you to your cell, Nathan," said Gus, leaning back in his chair. "we'll be back after we've spoken to Grant Pearce and his boys."

"Another fishing expedition," sneered Nathan as he left the interview room with his escort.

"We've got the killer's car," Gus called after him, "a tango red Ford Fiesta. Imagine if we found a cellmate of Grant Pearce's who remembered a photograph of his boys with that car on his cell wall?"

Luke and Gus were alone in the room.

"Is that likely, guv?" asked Luke.

"Didn't you ask yourself why it only turned up three years ago by accident in that clocking scam? The killer used that car when he went to kill Dennis Gates and thought so much of it he couldn't get rid of it. If you accept that, then it's not much of a stretch to imagine the family photo album having several pictures of the said son with his pride and joy."

"It makes sense. The sons were the right age for the image of the killer we saw on CCTV. So how did they discover that Danny was now Dennis?"

"When we learned the names of five likely lads from Trefor Davies, we heard that Grenville was the only one enjoying a spell of freedom. Lydia informed us where Moira was serving her sentence. We'll find out where he is and visit Grant first to run the facts we have by him. I'll mention this visit in passing and then tell him how things developed after meeting Nathan Tatum. If he assumes Nathan filled in gaps in our knowledge, so be it. I want to see his reaction when we show him how much we know."

"Isn't that dangerous, guv?"

"Risk and reward, Luke. We're nearly there. It was one of the two lads. Before we tackle them, I'd like to know who realised Dennis Gates was the older version of the young man in the photo."

"That's easy, guv," said Luke, "William takes after his father in looks and stature. I haven't seen the football team photo, but I wouldn't mind betting they'd pass for brothers."

"I was in the Frayling-Gates house too, you know," said Gus, "did you think I overlooked the family photographs? The similarity is obvious. I need to know whether Nathan Tatum heard of the link from Grant Pearce. Did Pearce act alone, or did Tatum order the hit?"

"I get it now. Where next, guv?"

"Back to the office, Luke. There's enough time left in the day to arrange these visits. We may not get to the last of

them until Friday, but with a following wind, we'll have this
tied up by the end of the week."

Luke wondered if that was optimistic.

The skies were brighter now; Gus hoped that was a
good sign. Tatum accused him of fishing. It was something
he rarely resorted to doing. But, on this occasion, it was a
means to an end. He had Dennis Gates's killer in his sights.

Gus smiled to himself. It was an open goal that he
couldn't miss.

Chapter Twelve

Thursday, 31 May 2018

THE DAY of Terry Davis's funeral had arrived. Clouds shrouded the warm sun they'd enjoyed earlier in the week. At least the showery rain had gone. Gus waited in his kitchen for the team to arrive.

Luke drove to Urchfont from the other side of Devizes. Alex Hardy collected Lydia on his way through Chippenham. Gus wondered whether she had spent the night with him. Who was he to criticise?

Gus put any issues between him and Alex aside today. Instead, they would present a united front for Neil. Lydia kept Gus up to date with Alex's progress, which was acceptable for the time being.

Gus spotted a familiar face standing by the entrance to the West Wilts Crematorium. Clemency Bentham was in charge of the funeral service. She greeted Gus with her usual smile.

"I must remember to get my facts straight today, Mr

Freeman," she said, "with the county's finest in attendance. I've never seen so many polished silver buttons in my life."

"Terry was a rogue in many ways," said Gus, "but he was one of us and didn't deserve to die in the manner he did. My only regret is that we haven't yet caught up with his killer. He's a hard man to find."

"Justice will be done in the end," she said. Gus moved past her and sat next to the rest of his team. Neil and his mother followed the coffin. There was no sign of Melody.

Gus checked who was in the rows of seats ahead of them. The ACC, Geoff Mercer and the other senior officers had come. So it was no surprise that the Chief Constable and the Police and Crime Commissioner stayed away. Terry Davis wouldn't have wanted them there, anyway.

There were plenty of faces elsewhere in the room that Gus remembered meeting in the old days. Retired officers from Swindon and Salisbury mingled with serving officers across the county. Donna was there too, looking resplendent in an expensive coat and hat. You could mistake her for a minor Royal if you didn't know how she'd earned money to pay for it.

Gus spotted Vera at the back, but she didn't see him with her head bowed.

After the service, everyone walked the line to express their condolences to Terry's widow and Neil. Gus always felt this dragged out an already painful experience. For most of Terry's ex-colleagues and friends, the sooner they got to the pub to have a drink in his memory, the better. Gus recalled Neil telling him his Dad left more than enough for the purpose. He wondered which of the many bars Terry had visited was to benefit from the extra custom.

Gus reached the few family members able to attend the service.

"Thanks for coming, guv," said Neil after Gus had spoken with his mother.

"How's Melody?" asked Gus.

"As well as can be expected," said Neil, "she couldn't face this. So I'm hoping things will pick up after today. I want to say I'll be back next week, but I don't know."

"When you're both ready, Neil," said Gus, "where are you going later?"

"The Three Crowns, to begin with, guv. Can you join us?"

"Alex and Lydia might drop in for a while. Luke and I are interviewing a witness."

"I'm missing that buzz," said Neil, "are you close to getting your man?"

"If you mean in our cold case, Neil, then yes, we are. As for Warwickshire Police finding Ricky Gardiner, well, the hunt continues. I hoped to bring good news today, but it wasn't possible."

"Never mind, he can't hide forever."

"Luke and I will head to Bristol, then. I'll raise a glass to Terry's memory this evening when I get home."

"Thanks, guv. Good hunting."

Luke joined Gus shortly after, and they made their way through the trees to the car park.

"First stop, HMP Bristol and Grant Pearce," said Gus. "You would think as he closes in on his sixtieth birthday, he'd realise crime doesn't pay, wouldn't you?"

"You can't educate pork, so they say," said Luke. He started the engine and made his way towards the main gates.

The interview with the head of the Pearce family was much as Gus expected. Grant Pearce swaggered into the interview room as if he owned it. Gus had primed Luke on the drive to Horfield to make the necessary introductions and explain why they needed to speak with him.

Pearce listened to Luke's spiel but never took his eyes off Gus. Perhaps someone got a message to him, warning him to be on his guard.

Gus thought he'd take the risk.

"We can only explain the murder of Dennis Gates by turning back the clock. First, let's return to 1998. Do you recall where you were, Grant? I'll refresh your memory. It was HMP Dorchester. You shared a cell with Nathan Tatum, a nasty piece of work. Nathan was eleven when his sister Gemma ran away with a youngster named Danny Giles. We visited Nathan yesterday for a chat. He was most helpful. Nathan was adamant justice wasn't served when Giles left prison after only three years. But you knew that, didn't you? If we go back to 1985, by coincidence, you were at HMP Lewes while Danny Giles was there. When Nathan showed you a photograph of the young assistant coach to his sister's football team in Dorchester, blow me if it wasn't a lad you remembered from Lewes. You discussed your families and the rights and wrongs of life in general. Nathan wanted his revenge no matter how long it took. You agreed to search for Danny Giles. Who knows? Did Nathan Tatum ask several other inmates from different parts of the country to do the same over the years? Either way, anyone Nathan persuaded to help in his quest was after the wrong man. Danny Giles ceased to exist within weeks of leaving Lewes prison. He reverted to the name his birth mother gave him."

Grant Pearce still stared at Gus. He did not comment.

"I gather you know DI Trefor Davies in Marlborough?" asked Gus, "he's been in town for a while. One thing Trefor excels at is compiling data for a murder file. Often much of it proves useless. A detective reviewing the evidence during the original investigation summarised what was in a packet of data and carried it forward, hoping to avoid ploughing through the lot if he searched for a random fact or image. I flicked through his summary, which confirmed what a great bloke Dennis Gates was and that he was a regular sponsor for the local football club where his son, William, was a leading player. Dennis's was one of several businesses that paid for the club's match balls. The local paper carried a report on the new season due to start in early September. On the sports page was a photograph of the club captain being handed the ball for the last Home game of the previous campaign. 'Prominent businessman Dennis Gates presents the match ball to his son, William.' There they were, father and son, side by side, smiling for the camera. Dennis was now forty-nine, but William bore the same traits at fifteen. A quick check of the strip of photograph Nathan Tatum let you have in prison at Dorchester was enough to seal Dennis's fate."

"I was in prison in August 2010," said Grant Pearce, "I don't know what lies that Tatum bloke spun you, but it couldn't have been me."

"Nathan Tatum was inside too. Neither of you did it. We know who did. We've got your son's car," said Gus, "the tango red Ford Fiesta. Would it surprise you that someone remembered a photograph of your son with that car on a cell wall?"

Luke sprang to his feet. The prison officer was slower to react but recovered in time to help prevent Grant Pearce from scrambling across the table to attack Gus. Luke and the officer sat Pearce back in his seat and stood close by him.

"Grenville's a bloody fool," said Grant, "I told him to

nick a car to do the job, but no, he had to drive his precious Fiesta. As soon as I heard, I told him to get rid of it. He swore he dumped it with a group of lads on a Swindon housing estate. The police found no evidence worth having at the time—nothing on the car, the gun, or the shooter. We laughed ourselves silly. Grenville got away with it. He's a lucky sod."

"When did you contact Nathan?"

"As soon as I saw the newspaper. I got a message to Tatum at Whitemoor on Saturday, the day after the local paper came out. He sent me a reply, just four words. Do him for me."

"What did you say to Grenville?"

"I told him everything Nathan told me about Danny Giles, how he targeted young girls and had sex with them. I told him how he'd abused Nathan's sister and forced her to run away with him. Grenville was fine after that. He couldn't wait to kill a paedophile."

"Thank you, Grant," said Gus, "that explains the last piece of the puzzle. Dennis's son, William, heard Grenville shout something as he fired the two shots. Paedo was the word muffled by the noise of the gun. Don't make any plans. We'll be back."

The prison officer escorted Grant Pearce from the room. The officer turned right to return Pearce to his cell. Luke and Gus followed behind and then turned left along a passageway to the entrance.

"We can forget interviewing Gordon Pearce then, guv? Do we arrest Grenville now?"

"No, Luke, we're heading to the office. I'll call Trefor Davies when we get there, and he can make the arrest. It was his work that gave us the breakthrough. Once I saw the wood for the trees in that gargantuan murder file, it was obvious."

"What will happen to Nathan Tatum and Grant Pearce?" asked Luke.

"We can leave DI Davies to work that one out. We have Grant's statement on tape that he got his son, Grenville, to kill Dennis Gates on Nathan Tatum's behalf. Nathan ordered the hit. Do him for me. That could take more work, but Grant might give Trefor more details if he thinks he can cut a deal."

"Grant Pearce is getting on, guv," said Luke. "If he gets another long stretch, he could die in prison."

"Grant will look for something to bargain with then, won't he? His final deal."

Friday, 1 June 2018

EVERYTHING FELT FRESHER and brighter this morning. The warm weather was back as Gus drove to the office. He remembered the gloomy start to yesterday at Terry Davis's funeral and then the gradual increase in the size of that pinprick of light at the end of the tunnel. The Dennis Gates murder didn't have a gangland connection; it was about football. It was always football. If Gus had been interested in sport as a lad, it might have dawned on him earlier.

As well as the newspaper clipping, Gus found an article on Dennis Gates in a trade magazine from 1988 deep in the murder file. Dennis had given a brief, sanitised version of his childhood, omitting the name change. A detective had earmarked it for checking at a later date. But, unfortunately, the gangland connection intervened, and nobody followed up to see if the background was watertight.

"Morning, guv," said Lydia as he exited the lift.

"How was the wake in the Three Crowns?" asked Gus.

"A place packed with strangers," she replied, "most of the London Road contingent drank across the road in the White Bear. Alex didn't want to stay too long. So we left at six o'clock."

"The funeral party didn't arrive until noon," said Gus, "I admire your stamina. Heaven knows what time the others found their way home."

Luke was next through the lift door.

"Is Lydia up to date, guv?" he asked.

"Not yet, Luke; I was waiting for you."

"Did you make progress yesterday afternoon?" asked Lydia.

"We can tidy our desks of the Dennis Gates saga," said Gus. "The killer was Grenville Pearce, twenty-one at the time. Grenville was always dense and a hothead. His father fed him the idea that Danny Giles was a child molester and he deserved to die. So Grenville did what his father asked. I don't think Grenville knew Nathan Tatum ordered the hit from his prison cell in Whitemoor."

"Those scraps of information I texted you concerning the overlapping prison sentences did the trick then, guv?" said Lydia clapping her hands, "well done, you two."

"A team effort, as always, Lydia," said Gus. "I'm passing the ball to Trefor Davies now. He can make the arrest and complete the details for the Crown Prosecution Service."

"What was the story behind the Ford Fiesta, guv? Where was it between the day of the murder and the clocking gang raid?"

"That was easy enough," said Luke, "Grenville hung

onto it for a while because he was a boy racer at heart. Then, when he realised it could come back to bite him, he dumped it in Swindon. Neil suggested it was a company car, didn't he? The car got used and abused for years by the teenage gangs, and then something broke that needed repair. The current user probably took it into the garage days before the raid."

"That was a stroke of luck," said Lydia, "I do have something DI Davies might enjoy. After sending you the text message, I spent the rest of my day on social media. I checked accounts belonging to Craddock, Smith, Raymond and the Pearce brothers. There wasn't a photo of anyone on the front at Weymouth, guv. Grenville preferred Weston-super-Mare, Brean Sands and Savernake Forest. I've got a file of photos with him and his tango red Ford Fiesta in the Freeman Files."

"Icing on the cake, Lydia, well done," said Gus, "I took the liberty of suggesting to Nathan Tatum and Grant Pearce that someone might recall a photo on a cell wall. I was economical with the truth, but neither man denied that such photos ever existed. So we can add another case to the win column."

"What's next, guv?" asked Luke.

"I'll talk to Trefor Davies after I've updated the Freeman Files. He can have everything we have, including Lydia's photos. Then I'd better head to London Road to tell them the news."

"We'll start the tidy-up once you've left us, guv," said Luke.

"I have two questions, guv," said Lydia.

Gus looked up from his computer.

"Who's dealing with Annie and William Frayling-Gates, and what about Christine Gates?"

"There are several loose ends, Lydia," said Gus, leaning back in his chair. "I'll remind you of what I said when we solved the first of these cold cases. Our job is to find the killer. We've done that. It's over to others now to take the evidence we pass them, add more if required by re-interviewing the guilty party and pertinent witnesses and preparing for the court case. We should walk away. Another day, another collar, as Neil says. What did you think we should do?"

"When Annie and William learn the details of Dennis's past, it will be a terrible shock."

"The Dennis Gates they knew and loved wasn't a fraud, Lydia," said Gus. "Dennis was genuine. His crime was to fall in love with a girl under sixteen. Dennis paid his debt to society and, from then on, led a blameless life. I hope Annie and William can accept his decision to keep his past secret and move on with their lives."

"Dennis died because of bigots like Nathan Tatum and the Pearce family," said Luke, "there are still decent people in this world, thank goodness. I think your idea might be worth pursuing, Lydia."

"What was that?" asked Gus.

"I wondered whether we should put Annie and William in touch with Christine Gates. They met her without knowing how she connected to Dennis. She's alone in the world over there in Ventnor, with just a collection of cards, letters and photos to remember her son."

"We won't make a habit of it," said Gus, "but once the dust settles on this case, I reckon someone could find a way for those three to find one another. Can I leave that with you, Lydia?"

"It will be my pleasure, guv," she replied.

GUS LEFT the CRT office a few minutes before eleven. He'd updated the files, given the good news to a thankful Trefor Davies, and called the ACC to arrange an appointment. Kenneth Truelove and Geoff Mercer would be waiting with bated breath.

Thirty-five minutes later, he was climbing the stairs of the Wiltshire Police HQ.

Geoff stood at the top, waiting.

"Good news, I hear?"

"The best this week," said Gus.

Geoff tapped and entered the ACC's office. He turned from the window and sat at his desk.

"How on earth you found the time to tackle the Gates case this week, Freeman, let alone solve it, I don't know," said the ACC.

"Teamwork," replied Gus.

"Do we have our ducks in a row?"

"We do," said Gus, "we left Trefor Davies with a loose end or two. I hope it's enough for him to salve his conscience. All things considered, a satisfactory outcome."

"I'll pass you the murder file from your next case before you leave," said the ACC, "please don't look at it until Monday morning. There isn't a constant supply of these, you know?"

"What news on the other front?" asked Gus.

"Everything's in the hands of the IOPC, and they're confident we've provided sufficient evidence for a conviction," said the ACC.

"Have they spoken with Her Majesty yet?"

"Not yet, nor have they been in touch with Dominic Culverhouse. I expect action early next week. The Chief Constable has left for the weekend. Vera passed the information on when she and Kassie Trotter did the coffee rounds mid-morning. A quiet weekend with her partner, Naomi. Hall, I imagine."

"I'd be surprised if they aren't aware something's in the wind," said Geoff Mercer.

"Just one more headache to solve then," said Gus.

"I spoke with Oliver Pinnock yesterday evening," said Geoff, "it's only a matter of time. The net is closing. They've liaised with the Met and checked out Gardiner's known hiding places. Similar to the other affair, they expect to make an arrest early next week."

"How are your resources?" asked the ACC, "will DS Davis return to work next week? What's happening with DS Hardy too?"

"We're coping," said Gus, "Luke Sherman and Lydia work well together. But, I won't deny we could use another pair of hands."

"I received a message from DI Carlton from Royal Leamington Spa," said Geoff Mercer. "Andy's got a Detective Constable looking to transfer to a station closer to her parents. They're moving to Bath in the next few weeks, where her father will take up a lecturer's position at the University."

"Another female, is she any good?" asked Gus.

"DC Blessing Umeh is young, keen and ambitious to work with you before you retire for good," said Geoff.

"The poor, deluded girl. I can't see Neil and Alex rushing back in the next week or two. We'll have to return Luke to his real job before long, so why not? If the ACC is happy for us to have a bigger team, I'm not complaining."

"He's setting you up for the time when Lydia gets moved onwards and upwards," said Geoff.

"I'm not the villain here," said Kenneth Truelove. "Her Majesty has hovered over me ever since she arrived, questioning numbers and the logic of having Gus here in the first place. If everything goes to plan, we'll have another new Chief Constable. It's selfish of me, but I want to keep this unit performing with distinction until I retire. I want to leave on a high."

"After that, you couldn't care less," said Gus.

"Exactly," grinned the ACC. He selected a folder from his desk.

"Mark Malone died on the twelfth of May 2015. He drove his grey 5-series BMW with blacked-out windows into Devizes from the Beckhampton straight at around midnight. Someone fired six shots with a handgun. Malone lost control of his car and hit several parked vehicles before ending up in a garden. He got hit twice in the head and died in the hospital in Swindon at three fifty-five. That's your next case. Now forget it until after the weekend."

"I suppose I could get off home now?" said Gus, tucking the file under his arm. "I'll call the gang and tell them to finish clearing the decks before taking the rest of the day off."

"Enjoy the weekend, Gus," said Geoff when they left the ACC's office, "by the way, I need time before I can arrange this young DC's transfer. So you must soldier on with the three of you next week."

"No problem," said Gus. His eyes swept the first-floor admin area—no sign of familiar faces.

"Suzie Ferris hopes to return on Monday," said Geoff.

"She has a mind of her own, that one. I told her to rest, but these youngsters won't listen, will they? They think they're indestructible."

"Off you go, Gus. Take care."

Gus trotted downstairs and drove home to the bungalow. Despite the advice given to him by the ACC, he wanted to spend a few hours rifling through the murder file.

His best-laid plans came to nothing. Before he had time to change into casual gear, the front doorbell rang. It was Suzie.

Gus woke to the sound of a phone ringing in the lounge. He glanced at the clock as he walked through the hallway.

It couldn't be seven so soon. Gus recognised the number.

"Are you free this weekend?" asked Vera.

"I've nothing planned that can't change," said Gus.

"I'm collecting the keys to my new place at nine o'clock tomorrow morning. My father's organised a removals firm to move my stuff out of the cottage at eight. I'm spending the night at home. I couldn't face getting up at the crack of dawn."

"So you've spent your last night at the old place?" said Gus. "It holds happy memories."

"There'll be plenty of opportunities to create new memories in my new home," said Vera.

"Where do you need me, and at what time?"

"Parking will be an issue with the removal van there. Why don't you park on London Road and walk? I expect to see you striding towards my new front door at half-past nine."

"Have you got emergency supplies to take with you?"

"Of course," said Vera, "A kettle, a jar of coffee, choco-late biscuits for the removals men. Kassie's buns for you and me."

"I'll pick up a carton of milk from the Community Shop before I leave Urchfont."

"Thanks, Gus, for offering to help. I know you're busy."

"No problem," said Gus, "what are friends for?"

"I wonder whether she knew I was here?" asked Suzie after Gus ended the call.

"What will you do now?" asked Gus.

"I hope you won't kick me out first thing. You can spend a day lifting and carrying Vera's worldly possessions. I'll drive home, ride, and then rest, just like the doctor ordered. I can be here when you get back."

"You've got it all sorted out, haven't you?" sighed Gus.

"I wish I did, Gus," said Suzie leading him towards the bedroom, "but I looked up that Kierkegaard fellow you mention to see if I could find something to help."

Gus thought for a second.

"The greatest danger in a man's life is not to take the risk."

"That's the one," said Suzie.

vinci-books.com/barkingmad

One fugitive, one team—can justice prevail against the odds?

In May 2015, the peaceful life of Mark Malone, a beloved pet-shop owner, was shattered by a deadly storm of bullets. Poised against the notorious fugitive Ricky Gardiner, Freeman and his Crime Review Team embark on a relentless pursuit that tests their resolve and determination to bring a killer to justice.

Turn the page for a free preview…

Barking Mad: Chapter One

Monday, 4 June 2018

Gus Freeman arrived at the Old Police Station office a few minutes before nine o'clock. Was it possible so much had happened since last Monday morning? Where had those quiet, lazy days of retirement disappeared?

Seven days ago, he'd made the journey from his bungalow in Urchfont to the London Road HQ, looking forward to a new work week. But, instead, his Crime Review Team faced the prospect of a new case in which to immerse themselves. The mystery they were to grapple with was why on earth car dealer Dennis Gates died at the hands of a lone assassin back in September 2010.

Gus thought he'd spend the coming week searching for new witnesses, opening new lines of enquiry, and finding answers to the questions that remained after the initial investigation.

Today should have been the start of a second week on

the case that might bring those different threads to a satisfying, neat conclusion.

Those well-intentioned plans melted away within a minute of walking through the Wiltshire Police building's main doors. However, Gus could still hear Ricky Gardiner's chilling message, "Suzie Ferris dies if you open your mouth."

Within the hour, his superiors took decisive action.

Kenneth Truelove, the Assistant Chief Constable, agreed to block any attempt by the Chief Constable to interfere in the smooth running of the CRT. He would convince Her Majesty that nothing had changed. Work on the new cold case was the Crime Review Team's sole priority. The ACC would ensure Sandra Plunkett had no ammunition to use against Gus and his team.

Meanwhile, DS Geoff Mercer stepped away from his mainstream role, ostensibly due to a family emergency. Instead, he agreed to help Gus search for Suzie Ferris and gather evidence against the people behind her kidnapping.

As the lift took him to the first floor, Gus thought about how the past seven days had frazzled his team's nerves.

DS Alex Hardy was on gardening leave. The motorcycle pursuit rider had battled hard to return to work after a high-speed crash resulted in eighteen months of operations and recovery. Gus held Alex's reputation in high regard after the first two months they'd worked together. However, mistakes marred his work as the hunt for Suzie Ferris became more frantic.

Lydia Logan Barre suspected her lover used pills to mask the problems raised by accelerating the switch from wheelchair to crutches and finally from crutches to walking unaided. Gus had to face facts. Alex was unavailable until he conquered his demons. With Lydia's help, he would return to the fold in time.

So should DS Neil Davis. When things go wrong, they can go wrong big-time. No sooner had Neil resumed his place in the CRT office after his father's murder than his wife Melody suffered a miscarriage. Gus had no idea how traumatic an event a miscarriage could prove for the young couple, but he had enough sense to know Neil shouldn't rush. The team would welcome him back with open arms when he was ready to resume work.

As the lift doors opened, only two faces looked towards him. Lydia gave her usual smile. DS Luke Sherman nodded a silent greeting. These two then were the new, slim-line version of the Crime Review Team until further notice.

"Good morning, guv," said Lydia, "we're all set for the new case. Did you collect the murder file last Friday?"

"I did," said Gus, "and the ACC told me to forget it until today. I think the ACC believed we'd had a week packed with incidents, and it was only fair we took time to draw breath."

"We arrived two minutes before you, guv," said Luke. "The Freeman Files are up-to-date and can go to London Road once you've checked through them and added your contributions."

"Thanks, Luke," said Gus, "Leave that with me. You two can clear the decks ready for action on our next case. Please keep your fingers crossed we don't have any nasty surprises waiting for us. Last week provided us with more than enough."

"At least you had a quiet weekend, guv," said Lydia, "did you spend most of it tending to your allotment?"

"I squeezed in a visit," said Gus. He concentrated on the computer screen before him, hoping Lydia got the message he wanted to avoid further conversation regarding the weekend.

"Did you find out how DI Ferris is, guv?" asked Lydia.

Gus knew it wasn't an unreasonable question. Along with help from Geoff Mercer and WPC Amelia Cranston, his team helped bring Suzie home unharmed. Of course, everyone wanted to know how she was faring.

"We spoke over the weekend," he said. "Suzie is young, mentally strong, and although the doctors signed her off until the end of this week, it wouldn't surprise me if she made it into London Road earlier."

That seemed to satisfy the inquisitive young Scot. Gus glanced over the top of his monitor and saw Lydia wiping the first of the whiteboards.

Gus let the cursor on his computer hang for a while as he considered the quiet weekend Lydia believed he'd enjoyed.

Saturday morning was the first test of the new arrangement for Gus Freeman.

He'd woken at half-past seven to the sound of Suzie singing in the shower. She'd kept her word and allowed him to have a good night's sleep. Gus got out of bed and wandered in his boxer shorts to the kitchen. He needed sustenance. A bowl of cornflakes wasn't enough to set him up to move Vera Butler's furniture for a day. A proper cooked breakfast was in order. He started brewing the coffee.

"Good morning, sleepyhead," said Suzie.

Gus did a double-take at the youthful woman standing in the doorway.

A towel wrapped around her head was fair enough. The shirt that barely covered the essentials was the same one Vera donned the first time she stayed the night.

He had to agree it looked better on them than it ever did on him.

"I hope you don't mind," said Suzie, "it looked unloved hanging in your wardrobe, and my things are still in my car."

"I should have popped out to get your bag. I'm sorry."

"Don't go dressed like that. You'll get arrested."

"I was about to say the same to you."

"One of us needs to go," said Suzie. "Shall I cook breakfast while you shower and get dressed? It will be ready by the time you've done that and retrieved my things."

"What can I look forward to?" Gus had asked.

"As close to a full English as I can achieve with whatever's in that fridge of yours," said Suzie.

Gus had headed for the shower. This new arrangement was off to a promising start. Gus found no reason to change his opinion after they had eaten.

"That was scrumptious," said Suzie, "even if I say it myself."

"You're a woman of many talents," said Gus.

"I'm looking forward to riding out in the country," said Suzie, looking up at near-cloudless skies through the kitchen window.

"Can we squeeze another cup of coffee out of that percolator?" asked Gus.

"Half a cup each," said Suzie, "you can't put it off much longer. Vera needs you on duty by nine. After this coffee, it will be time to get into that car of yours and head into town. I must be off too."

They left the bungalow together at a quarter to nine and headed in opposite directions. Suzie headed for her stable in Worton. After dropping into the Community Shop for milk, Gus drove to London Road. He agreed with Vera that a quick walk to her new home was preferable to a forlorn search for a place to leave his car.

Gus parked in Geoff Mercer's bay and set off along the road. He was fifty yards from his destination when he heard someone calling his name. He recognised the voice.

"Morning, Mr Freeman."

"Good morning, Kassie," said Gus, turning to watch the young woman trot across the road carrying two heavy bags.

Some things never changed. Kassie's mop of hair now sported an orange streak, and the sleeveless top allowed her known tattoos to appear in public. Kassie wobbled to a halt next to him and caught her breath. Gus couldn't detect any added piercings.

"I've brought supplies," Kassie gasped.

"Have you been drafted in to help, too?" asked Gus, holding a hand to take one of her heavy bags.

"Thanks," said Kassie, handing over a bag, "yes, Vera asked me in the week if I was free."

"What on earth have you got in here, Kassie," he exclaimed, "it weighs a ton."

"I think I brought far too much grub. Vera's got the drinks covered, but workers can be greedy devils. I brought every type of baked goods I had in the house to be on the safe side. I can always take it back."

"I'll run you home afterwards," said Gus, "you could do yourself a mischief."

"Run me home?" asked Kassie. "Oh, it's true then. Vera said last week that you two weren't love's young dream these days. I thought you and Vera would christen her new home."

Gus gave Kassie a stern look.

"Vera and I are best friends, Kassie," said Gus, "I don't think either of us ever imagined it becoming more serious."

"Friends with benefits," said Kassie.

"None of your business, young lady," said Gus.

"All right for you," she said.

"Still no sign of your own Jon Snow then, Kassie?"

Kassie sighed.

"Perhaps, I should stop baking and find a hobby that isn't food-related."

"Here comes Vera," said Gus as her yellow Alfa Romeo turned the corner and parked at the end of the cul-de-sac.

A large removals van trundled into sight. Let the games begin.

"Hello, you two," said Vera, "sorry if you've been waiting long. The boys were late arriving."

"Kassie kept me company," said Gus.

Vera kissed him on the cheek and handed him another bag to carry.

"Everything we need to keep us in coffee or tea throughout the day's in there. Pop the milk in on top. There's just enough room."

Kassie was otherwise engaged. Her attention was on the removal men. Four well-built youths were preparing to unload the contents of the van.

Vera led the way to the front door. Gus followed her, hoping the handles of the bags lasted another ten strides. He heard Kassie puffing her way up the path behind him.

"Did you catch that testosterone, Mr Freeman? Today might not be a complete disaster."

Gus smiled. Hope springs eternal.

Six hours later, the move was complete, and the removals van returned to base.

Many of Kassie's buns got admired and devoured, and copious amounts of coffee were drunk. Vera was happy that nothing had got broken, and apart from a few minor adjustments after everyone had left, she could have everything where she planned.

"Thank you for today," said Vera, handing a glass of champagne to Gus and Kassie.

"What are friends for?" said Gus.

"I burp after I've drunk a sip or two of this," said Kassie, collapsing onto the nearest comfortable chair.

"Do you have to rush away, Gus?" asked Vera.

"Mr Freeman offered to give me a lift because of what I needed to carry," said Kassie. "Although with the grub those removals guys put away, I could manage on the bus. I'll need to bake again tomorrow to replenish my stocks."

"Yes," said Gus, "you wouldn't want to run out of supplies for Geoff Mercer's teatime snacks halfway through the week."

Kassie burped.

"Told you," she said.

"What about you, Gus?" asked Vera.

"I don't think I can compete with that, sorry."

Vera laughed.

"No, I mean, do you have to be somewhere?"

"Not for an hour or two," he said. "When Kassie's ready, I'll run her home to Worton."

"It's been a long day," said Vera. "I'll call my parents and persuade them to pop over later. I know my father wants to check he got good value for the money he paid that removals firm. After my parents leave, I reckon it will be an early night."

Kassie and Gus shared a look. He wondered whether Kassie expected him to return here as soon as he'd dropped her in the village.

"You chose well, Vera," said Gus, changing the subject and looking around the living room. "This place is a few minutes from work and next to the town centre. Moreover, it's compact enough to allow you to put your stamp on it without stretching the budget."

"It's ideal for one person," said Kassie, "it's the type of place I hope to get one day. You'll be happy here."

"Sure, I will," said Vera, "do you two want a coffee before you head home?"

"I couldn't drink another cup," said Gus.

"I'll risk another glass of bubbly," said Kassie, "and then we'll go home."

Thirty minutes later, Gus and Kassie made their way up London Road to the HQ's car park.

"Do I need to ask?" asked Kassie as she sat in the passenger seat with a bump.

"What?" asked Gus. "Where did I have to be in an hour? Suzie Ferris went riding today, and we loosely arranged that she would drop by the bungalow early this evening. We might grab a quick bite in the Lamb. Who knows?"

"Do you honestly believe that Vera's cool with how things have turned out?" asked Kassie.

"I stopped trying to work out how a woman's mind works a long time ago, Kassie," said Gus. "Whatever happens, I don't want anyone to get hurt, myself included."

Kassie was half-asleep before they reached the front of the old Rising Sun pub. Gus had to agree; it had been a long day. He pulled up and parked the Focus.

"Here we are, Kassie," he said, giving her a nudge.

"Enjoy your evening, Mr Freeman," she said, "do nothing I wouldn't like to do. See you on Monday, no doubt."

With that, Kassie grabbed her bags and headed for a gap in the hedge. Gus caught sight of a flash of orange hair behind the barrier and heard the house's front door, where she rented a room, slam shut.

Gus drove away from Worton and made for Urchfont. He checked his watch as he neared the bungalow; it was a quarter past five. If the driveway was empty, he could spare an hour to contemplate life on his allotment. There was no sign of Suzie yet.

The longer June days brought more sunshine and time to be gardening. Gus expected to see Bert Penman in his usual spot, but he found both patches of ground on either side of his allotment deserted.

It was Saturday, and Clemency Bentham had a busy day ahead. Perhaps this was the time she wrote her sermons. As for Bert, either he was in the Lamb, or he'd taken produce across to Irene North. There was plenty to choose from at present. Cabbage, cauliflower, and broad beans were ready to harvest now. Gus could see salad items that Irene might enjoy too. His lettuce, spring onion and radish plants looked ready to take to the table.

Gus studied his early potatoes and wondered how he had the cheek to call them his. Bert had done the lion's share of the work. Still, they needed lifting in a fortnight.

Gus decided he'd get on with the one job he could do without checking with Bert. He fetched his hoe from the shed. Almost from the first day he'd taken on this piece of land, Bert had told him to hoe at every opportunity to remove weeds and break up the soil. When the showers came, they would, before you knew it, allow water to soak into the earth. Gus passed the next hour, hoeing, thinning out and watering.

He did a little thinking on the new case too. It was only Saturday, and he'd promised to hold off until Monday, but old habits die hard.

Mark Malone's BMW had tinted windows, a lowered suspension, and a loud car stereo. He drove it at speed along the Beckhampton straight late at night back in 2015. That wasn't unusual. It was hard to resist speeding on that stretch of road. Hundreds of drivers got caught speeding there every year in the old days. Several died in high-speed accidents.

The Malone incident was different because he'd stopped at a JET garage on the A4 in Bath Road, outside Marlborough, fifteen minutes earlier. A grey 7-series BMW stopped behind him, and the two drivers appeared to argue. The attack might have been a case of road rage or mistaken identity.

As Malone reached the outskirts of Devizes, someone fired six shots with a handgun. Malone lost control of his car and hit several parked vehicles before ending up in a garden. He got hit twice in the head and died in the hospital later that morning.

Malone lived in Bath and had driven from a friend's house in Newbury. The original investigation, headed by Gus's old acquaintance DI Trefor Davies found nothing in Malone's background to suggest his involvement in any criminal activity. The detectives working the case thought the reason for Mark Malone's murder was linked to the events before the shooting. There was no evidence of any long-running dispute with anyone in the Devizes area. There was little to suggest a targeted attack. Nobody could have anticipated Malone driving in that spot at that time.

Gus tried to figure out whether Devizes had any direct connection to the murder. Was it little more than a convenient spot between Newbury and Bath that presented itself to the gunman?

So far, he hadn't studied the murder file in depth. How

did Malone earn a living? He was a week short of his thirtieth birthday when he died. The flashy car suggested Malone wasn't short of money, but that didn't always follow. Like many other young, thrusting entrepreneurs, he could have been living beyond his means. That was something to check on Monday when they faced this case.

As Gus cleaned his hoe before putting it back in his shed, another thought struck him.

Malone's friends lived in Newbury. Why not head for the M4 and give that BMW a treat? Malone wouldn't have been the first driver to press the pedal to the metal and cover the fifty miles in half an hour without getting caught.

Gus knew he shouldn't encourage drivers to break the law, but seventy miles per hour always felt too restricting on a motorway in perfect driving conditions. Moreover, the numbskulls who drove at fifty through a built-up area when children were going home from school irked him.

He was lucky if his Ford Focus could reach fifty miles per hour these days, especially between home and work. Nevertheless, Gus convinced himself it wasn't the car's performance that stopped him; it was the constant traffic volume.

As he drove along the lane towards his bungalow at a sedate twenty miles per hour, he filed away another question to add to Monday's list. Why did Mark Malone travel across the county via the old A4 road to reach Bath? A route where the opportunities to give the powerful BMW a chance to show its paces were few and far between?

As he turned into his driveway, Gus noticed that Suzie had beaten him to it. He parked beside her GTI, and she got out to greet him.

"Miss me?" she said.

"Hard to say," said Gus, "I've been so busy. I hope you

haven't been waiting long. Nobody was here when I returned from Vera's, so I popped along to the allotment."

"Don't worry. I only arrived two minutes ago. How did the move go?"

"It went smoothly," said Gus, "we had four willing men to do the heavy work from the firm Vera's father employed. Kassie Trotter came along to help. She supplied everyone with food and drink. Vera couldn't trust her with her breakable items; you know what Kassie's like. I dropped her off in the village with the few scraps that remained of her baked goods. She'll have a full day in her little kitchen tomorrow."

Suzie smiled.

"What?" asked Gus.

"Didn't you find it odd that Vera invited Kassie?"

"I hadn't thought about it until you mentioned it. Vera and Kassie work together every day. It makes sense that Kassie offered to help, doesn't it?"

"What was Vera doing this evening?"

"She invited her parents over to view her new abode," said Gus. "I think I see where this is heading now. Vera asked around mid-afternoon whether I needed to dash off anywhere. I said, not for two hours. Vera didn't press matters, and I didn't elaborate. The three of us then drank a glass of champagne to toast the new home, and when Kassie was ready to leave, we walked up London Road to retrieve my car from Geoff Mercer's parking spot. You think Vera had Kassie in attendance to avoid any uncomfortable moments?"

"It worked, didn't it? I assume Kassie came into town on the bus, and you're too much of a gentleman not to offer her a lift home afterwards. Vera knew that. It meant you could disappear with a valid reason and not worry about later because you knew her parents were keeping her company."

"You've got it worked out, haven't you?" said Gus heading for the front door.

"I wouldn't assume to have all the answers, Gus," said Suzie, "how are you feeling, anyway?"

"It's been a tiring day," he said as they stood in the hallway.

"Have a shower, freshen up and get changed," said Suzie, "I'll keep busy until you're ready, and then we'll go somewhere for a meal. Nothing too heavy. I'll drive if you wish."

"We could walk to the Lamb," Gus suggested.

"That sounds like a better idea. We can both have a drink then."

Gus broke into his reverie to finish his contributions to the Dennis Gates case in the Freeman Files. Lydia and Luke would soon wonder when he would start discussing their new cold case.

"Coffee, guv?" asked Lydia, noticing her boss was no longer staring at his computer screen.

"Perfect timing," said Gus, "I'm almost done with the Gates files. Next, I want to run through the bare bones of the Malone case and select items for the Hub to process. The murder file we've received from the ACC looks thin compared to the previous one."

"Mark Malone was only twenty-nine, guv," said Lydia, "it's no age, is it?"

"You can say that again," said Luke, "he was only eighteen months older than me. The same age as Nicky, almost to the day, when he died in 2015."

Lydia was on her way to the restroom when Gus's phone rang.

"Please don't let this be another Blue Monday," said Gus.

"Good morning, Freeman."

It was Kenneth Truelove, the ACC.

"Good morning, Sir," said Gus, "how can I help?"

"I need you and Geoff Mercer in my office at ten o'clock. Don't be late."

Gus was about to reply when he realised the ACC had ended the call.

"Trouble, guv?" asked Luke.

"The ACC didn't give much away, Luke, but I guess there's a balloon somewhere, and it's still rising. I'll finish this last paragraph, and then I can deliver the files to him in person. Let's hope that reduces his stress levels."

Five minutes later, Lydia returned from the restroom with three cups of coffee to find Gus preparing to leave.

"Was it something I said, guv," she asked.

"Trouble brewing," said Luke, "Gus got the dreaded Monday morning call."

"What on earth has happened now?" sighed Lydia as her boss disappeared behind the lift door.

Gus reached the ground floor and exited the building. He threw his files onto the passenger seat and clipped on his seat belt. Here we go again. As Gus eased the Focus into traffic on the High Street, he resumed his thoughts of the weekend.

Saturday night was the first time he'd visited the Lamb with Suzie. He and Vera always went further afield, sometimes to places neither was well known. Vera was still married at the start of their relationship, so it made sense.

Things eased in the last few weeks, but that changed last Sunday after his confession.

As Gus walked through the pub door with Suzie on his arm, he recalled that he and Tess rarely used the place. He'd been here with Neil Davis for Frank North's wake; it wasn't uncommon for him to have a quick pint with Bert Penman after a session at the allotment.

It was a different matter to arrive with a woman half his age. Several heads turned their way, and conversation stalled for minutes rather than seconds.

"We've caused a stir," said Suzie, "our secret's out."

They had enjoyed a drink and a bar meal while chatting over the day's events. It was very civilised, Gus thought. With each passing minute, the Lamb's regulars lost interest in them, and when Suzie suggested they leave at ten o'clock, Gus didn't think anyone noticed.

Sunday was a leisurely day. Neither of them was in a rush to get out of bed. There were no pressing appointments, so Gus decided it required brunch. He worked in the kitchen while Suzie showered and dressed. After they had eaten, Suzie suggested a walk in the fresh air. They left the bungalow at two o'clock, and she drove them to Westbury. She and Gus climbed the hill near Bratton to enjoy the view and consider the history of the White Horse carved into the chalky grassland five centuries earlier.

"Another Sunday, another journey back in time," said Gus, "it's amazing the number of places I've never visited in this county despite living here all my life."

"Modern life isn't everything it's cracked up to be," said Suzie, "I've always wanted to slow down, take time to look around me, rather than speed by in the car. That's the joy of riding like I did yesterday. It would be healthier for you, too, instead of sitting by your garden shed when you want to mull over a case."

"Look, young lady, I still bear the bruises from that trip I took on horseback to your farm. I'm too old to start riding, thank you very much."

"Don't worry, I won't try to change you," said Suzie. "I fell for the grumpy retired detective. Come on, let's get back. You can cook me something delicious, and then I'll leave you to catch up on your sleep."

Later that evening, after Suzie drove home to Worton, Gus sat in the lounge with a large glass of Malbec. He watched nonsense on TV for an hour and then headed for the bathroom. There were a few additions besides his shower and bathroom cabinet items. Well, it made sense if Suzie planned to stay over regularly.

This morning, when he opened the wardrobe door to grab his pale blue work shirt and dark trousers, he had another surprise. He found his clothes squeezed into the right-hand side, just like the old days when Tess allowed him to occupy a fifth of the available space.

Since her death, Gus had spread his few clothing items along the rail so it didn't feel empty. Instead, he thought back to yesterday. He and Suzie dressed casually, and he got a polo shirt out of a drawer with the same pair of dark slacks he'd worn on Saturday evening.

The extra clothing must have been put in the wardrobe since he got home from Vera's. Of course, that was what Suzie was doing when she kept busy while he showered after returning from Vera's.

Did this mean Suzie was moving in bit by bit? Or was it just enough things to survive a weekend? If he weren't due to meet Geoff and the ACC to learn of yet another crisis, he would need to give the matter thought.

How did he feel about what it might mean?

One thing Gus was sure of as he bounded up the stairs to the administration area.

How quickly things could change.

Geoff Mercer spotted him from the other side of the room. He waved a hand, and Gus waved back. Vera and Kassie were on the coffee round. They had plenty of doors to knock on before they reached the ACC's office. Geoff Mercer joined Gus outside the door.

"Any idea what's happened?" asked Gus.

"Everyone's tight-lipped this morning," said Geoff, "it feels serious. I hope it's news of Gardiner's arrest."

Geoff knocked, and the ACC called them in. He sat at his desk.

"There's no way to soften the blow of this news, I'm afraid," he said. "We received a call this morning from Staffordshire Police. As you know, the Chief Constable left early on Friday to spend the weekend in the Midlands. She joined her partner, Naomi Hall, at their home near Lichfield. Yesterday evening a dog walker heard an engine running but couldn't see a nearby car. She realised the sound was coming from the garage."

"Dear God, no," said Geoff.

"She called the emergency services, and they opened the garage door. But it was far too late to save the occupants of the car, Sandra Plunkett and Naomi Hall."

"Was there a note?" asked Geoff.

"A tear-stained envelope addressed to the Staffordshire Chief Constable was inside the house," said the ACC, "not much detail in the letter. Sandra apologised to her family and colleagues for a serious error of judgement in the past. No names, no pack drill."

"Sandra Plunkett couldn't face the imminent disclosure

of the facts surrounding the hit-and-run she covered up with Dominic Culverhouse," said Gus. "She realised her career was over. The shame was too much to bear."

"There was worse to come if the IOPC linked her to Terry Davis's murder," said Geoff Mercer. "They can't follow the money trail until Gardiner gets arrested, but if she and Culverhouse paid him to murder Terry as we believe, then a loss of career was the least of her worries."

"What have we done?" asked the ACC. He stood and walked to the window.

"Our jobs," said Gus Freeman.

DS Geoff Mercer nodded his agreement.

Barking Mad: Chapter Two

It was noon before Gus drove back to the Old Police Station office.

Geoff Mercer persuaded Gus to stay with Kenneth Truelove until Vera and Kassie delivered the coffee and biscuits. After they left the room, the two friends attempted to calm the ACC's nerves.

"We did nothing wrong," said Geoff, "Culverhouse and Plunkett did."

"The evidence we passed to the IOPC was damning," agreed Gus, "Culverhouse and Plunkett have nobody to blame but themselves."

"What about Naomi Hall?" asked the ACC, "she didn't deserve to die."

"We have no idea how much she knew of the incident six years ago," said Geoff. "Naomi Hall came from Oakley, and she and Sandra lived together for years. If she was innocent, could she merely walk away when her lover admitted what would happen? Perhaps, but how could we anticipate a double suicide would be the outcome?"

"Who knows about the deaths?" asked Gus.

"The Police and Crime Commissioner," said the ACC.

"I bet that woke him up," said Gus, "he'll wish he did something less stressful. That's two Chief Constables he's seen disappear since I returned to work."

Kenneth Truelove gave Gus a look that suggested he thought this was Gus's fault.

"Who's taking charge in the interim?" asked Geoff.

"Why do you think I'm getting stressed?" said the Acting Chief Constable. "All I asked for was a quiet rundown to retirement. No major crimes, scandals, or headaches; not much to ask after forty years of faithful service."

"Life's hard, and then you die," said Gus.

"That bloody Kierkegaard fellow again, I presume?"

"Sorry, Sir, he can't get the blame for that one."

"When are you going to announce this to the troops?" asked Geoff.

"The media people are getting a speech prepared," said the ACC. "The IOPC investigation is in its early stages, and they have yet to interview Culverhouse. Ricky Gardiner is still at large. The PCC hopes to finish this with as little fuss as possible. I can't see how, but that's the way he wants to play it. The only people outside this office who know the genuine reason behind the deaths are the Staffordshire Chief Constable and our Police and Crime Commissioner."

"So, you'll inform everyone working for Wiltshire Police and the local media that the Chief Constable and her partner died in a tragic accident," said Gus. "Or words to that effect. The hope is it will buy the IOPC time to nail Culverhouse and arrest Gardiner. Both events are forecasted to occur early this week, anyway."

"Yes, the truth behind the double suicide will surface in

time," said the ACC, "they'll delay the post-mortem as long as they can. For two to three days. We're very much relying on others to do what's necessary. We can only sit and wait, not the situation I prefer."

Gus had to agree with him.

There was a knock at the door. The Police and Crime Commissioner walked into the room. He glanced towards Gus and Geoff.

"Our regular Monday meeting with the head of the Crime Review Team," said the ACC. Gus closed his eyes. It might have been better to say nothing. Now the PCC will suspect we were discussing the hush-hush news.

The PCC nodded and handed over a draft copy of the speech for the briefing and press release.

"We should discuss this," he said to the ACC.

Geoff and Gus got up to leave. They knew when they were surplus to requirements.

As the door closed behind them, Kassie Trotter grabbed Gus's arm.

"What's going on, Mr Freeman?" she asked, "we knocked on Her Majesty's door and found it locked. Vera tells me her car's not in the car park. Her Majesty was out of sorts last Friday. She wasn't as bitchy as usual. As if she'd had enough, you know?"

"You'll hear soon enough, Kassie. Don't fret. How's Vera?"

"Her parents loved the house when they dropped in on Saturday night. She had lunch with them in town some-where yesterday. It doesn't seem right when you and Vera aren't talking about one another, Mr Freeman. I had such high hopes for you two."

"I understand that, Kassie," said Gus. "You can't force

these things. Did any of those four lads from Saturday ask for your number?"

"Each of them did during the day," said Kassie. "I haven't heard from any of them yet, though. Typical."

"They don't know what they're missing, Kassie," said Gus, "you've got a heart of gold. So before I finish this consultancy, lark, I hope to see you meet Mr Right."

"I live in hope," sighed Kassie. "DI Ferris returns to work on Wednesday, Mr Freeman. Although I expect you heard that?"

"I did not," said Gus.

"Half days at first," said Kassie, "then if she copes with the pressure, Mr Mercer said she could return full time from next Monday."

"Excellent news," said Gus as he dashed downstairs and left the building

In the CRT office, Lydia and Luke were at a loose end. They couldn't progress the Mark Malone case without instructions from Gus Freeman. Luke had prepared a search routine for the Hub to process. He imagined they might need a list of drivers charged with road rage incidents.

"Why do we need that?" asked Lydia, "it was only a theory put forward by the detectives in the original investigation."

"While road rage is not an offence in UK law, many incidents occur because of dangerous or careless driving," said Luke Sherman. "All reports, whether or not damage or injury has occurred, can get considered. There could also be criminal penalties for assault or more serious offences against the person."

Gus Freeman overheard Luke's explanation as he emerged from the lift.

"Offences against the person? That's public order offences, Luke, am I right?"

"Yes, guv. I wondered if we should get the Hub to interrogate the records for drivers whose actions on the highway might likely cause harassment, alarm, or distress. Then, we might have an extensive list when we add it to drivers who got nicked for driving without due care and attention around the time of the Malone murder."

"What else will you be asking from the Hub?" asked Gus.

"I scraped the bottom of the barrel to get that much, guv, to be truthful," said Luke, "did you have any suggestions?"

Gus blew out his cheeks in frustration and flopped into his chair.

"Would you like a fresh coffee, guv?" asked Lydia.

"No, thanks," said Gus. "The news I received from London Road wasn't pleasant."

"Can you share it with us, guv?" asked Luke.

"The Chief Constable died at the weekend, together with her partner. They don't suspect foul play. That's the statement the media will get."

"That's dreadful," gasped Lydia.

"We mustn't blame ourselves," said Gus. "It fully justified the work that members of this team did to highlight the criminal wrongdoings of others. As hard as it is, we must move on."

Grab your copy…
vinci-books.com/barkingmad